The People's Friend

2022 Annual

Loch Lee, Angus

Nestled in the Angus Glens, within the Cairngorms National Park, is Loch Lee. Lying at the head of Glen Esk, and fed by the Water of Lee and the Water of Unich from the west and by the Water of Mark from the east, the loch acts as a reservoir, supplying drinking water to the local area.

It's a peaceful spot; you might hear the cry of a peregrine falcon or a golden eagle overhead. Queen Victoria described it as "a wild but not large lake, closed in by mountains, with a farmhouse and a few cottages at its edge", which doesn't really do justice to its natural beauty.

Despite its remote setting, there has been a parish church here for nearly 1,500 years. St Drostan initially founded the church. Over the centuries, the church was rebuilt several times, though the most recent, built in 1803, now stands about a mile away from the original, and holds only occasional services today.

The church remains a point of interest and reflection for the many tourists who visit the area to enjoy its walking routes, nature trails and birdwatching.

Contents

Dear Readers . . .

Welcome to "The People's Friend" Annual 2022! We have a real treat in store for you, with 25 brand-new short stories by some of your favourite authors, beautifully illustrated to bring the words to life.

There's a delightful selection of seasonal poems to enchant you, 10 stunning watercolour paintings from the brush of J. Campbell Kerr, and an armchair trip round some of Britain's most historic and impressive stately homes and castles.

I hope you enjoy it!

Angela

Angela Gilchrist, Editor

Complete Stories

Poetry

J. Campbell Kerr Paintings

Stately Homes And Castles

My Sunshine

by Teresa Ashby

THIS time last year you were still here, Mum.
Staying up till midnight so you could see in the New Year, then rushing to the back door as fast as your gammy knees would allow so you could fling it open and listen to the ships blowing in the harbour while fireworks went off all around, lighting up the night sky.

The next morning you would always be up before anyone else, eager to get the New Year off to the best possible start with a slap-up breakfast that no-one actually felt like eating after celebrating so late into the previous night.

But we soon found our appetites when we smelled the buttery croissants and sweet pastries.

But today I don't want to get up.

I don't want to start another year without you and your endless optimism. You were the life and soul of our family and I don't know how to carry on without you.

"It's like having a blank sheet of paper," you said every year. "You can write or draw anything you want."

"What are you going to write on yours?" I asked.

"Haven't decided yet," you said. "I'm still thinking about it. I do fancy an adventure, though."

All of life was an adventure with you, Mum.

As it turned out, last year you didn't get the chance to write anything on your sheet of paper. I couldn't believe you went so quickly and without warning.

It seemed that one minute you were there making us all crease up with your jokes and banter, and the next minute there was nothing but silence.

Nothing prepares you for the loss of your mother. You told me that. It was the one cloud in your sky, but you said I was the sunshine.

Illustration by Ruth Blair.

And suddenly I found myself in the same boat, and the one person I knew would understand had gone.

*　*　*　*

Valentine's Day was the first of the firsts. You always sent me a funny card. After Nan died I always gave you flowers, just like she had done, and you smiled and buried your nose in them.

I couldn't let it pass without doing something, so I got some flowers for Cassandra.

I thought she was going to roll her teenage eyes at me and groan, but she buried her nose in them just like you used to do.

Then she produced a card for me. It was so rude, but it made me laugh, probably for the first time since we lost you. It was the sort of card you would have bought.

I knew Mother's Day would be hard. I tried to prepare myself for it. All the shops were full of cards and gifts and big banners urging everyone to treat their mum.

I gave you flowers every Mother's Day, but last year I had to hurry past all the beautiful displays in the shops.

You can't block out the smell, though — and it was everywhere.

Cassandra gave me chocolates as always, but then she produced a huge bunch of flowers.

7

"They're for Granny," she said. "I thought we could put them on her grave."

"That's very sweet of you, love," I said, choking back the lump in my throat. "But the headstone hasn't been put in yet and there's nowhere to put any flowers."

"Then we'll take something," she said. "Come on. We can't not go and see Granny on Mother's Day."

You'd have been so proud of your granddaughter. She'd thought of everything. She even had a trowel in a bag so we could half bury a big jar for the flowers.

I still couldn't believe it, though, Mum. I couldn't get my head round the fact that I'd never see you again or hear that infectious laugh of yours.

I phoned you a few times because pressing your name on speed dial made me feel as if you were still there.

Then I'd listen to the message telling me the number I had dialled was not in use and my heart would break all over again.

Easter came next. You always bought me a little egg at Easter.

"For the child in you," you said. "Never let her go."

I used to give you a plant for your garden. Something with showy flowers that would attract the butterflies and bees you loved.

Cassandra stopped asking for chocolate eggs when she turned twelve, but last year I got her one. Just a little one, so she could hold on to her inner child.

She smiled and rubbed at her eyes and told me I was daft, but she gave me a plant. A primrose. I planted it in the garden and it's still alive, so I must have done something right with it.

Or maybe you've been watching over us, keeping an eye on things, making sure that nothing else dies.

I didn't want to get up on my birthday in May, but Cassandra came in with breakfast like she always used to when she was little.

She used to make me a cup of tea with water from the hot tap, do you remember? Because I'd always told her she wasn't allowed to boil the kettle.

There would be cold floppy toast, too, spread thickly with Marmite, but I'd eat it because that's what mums do, isn't it? I have to say her tea- and toast-making skills have improved a lot.

"Don't sit around in bed all day," she told me on my birthday. "I'm taking you out for lunch at the garden centre. But you'll have to drive, obviously."

That made me laugh. It's exactly what you used to say when you took me out for lunch at the garden centre.

Cassandra used to come, too, and we'd spend the afternoon choosing plants for the hanging baskets.

It seemed odd doing it without you, but Cassandra and I chatted and reminisced about your wonderful garden and how you always felt mine could do with rather more TLC than I gave it.

On your birthday in June, the tradition was that I always took you on a boat trip. Even Cassandra didn't miss it, although she often felt sea sick.

It didn't matter if that June day was bursting with sunshine or if it was grey and dull and pouring with rain, we went up the river, no matter what.

Last year, your birthday was hot. Hotter than I've ever known it. It would have been nice to go on a boat trip when the weather was so favourable.

I'd hardly even had that thought when Cassandra announced she'd booked us on a trip up the river.

Before we left, she picked a handful of sweet peas from the garden, and as we glided down the river, she scattered the flowers over the silky water.

She brought food for the swans, too, just like you used to.

On Cassandra's birthday in July, you always made her a lavish cake and covered it with whipped coconut cream and strawberries. We all loved it.

Cassandra used to say that cake was the best thing about having a birthday.

I'd kept the book where you wrote down all your favourite recipes and I tried to make Cassandra a birthday cake. It wasn't up to your standards, though. At least not to look at.

I couldn't get the coconut cream to whip up like you used to, but when we ate it we both said that, if we closed our eyes, we would have thought you'd made it.

August would have been your fortieth wedding anniversary.

You and Dad married late in your thirties and you always said you were both surprised when you got pregnant at the age of forty-two.

You joked about how hard it must be for me having "elderly parents", as you called it, but it wasn't hard at all. You were the best parents I could have asked for.

Even after Dad died, we continued to celebrate your wedding anniversary. For your fortieth we'd planned a barbecue with red heart-shaped balloons and table confetti.

It was going to be hard letting it pass, but as it turned out, I didn't have to.

Cassandra invited family and friends and arranged it all. We had the red heart-shaped balloons and we toasted you and Dad. You would have loved it.

September was the anniversary of Dad's death. You always took flowers to the cemetery on that day, but I didn't plan to.

I couldn't bear the thought of seeing the mound of earth.

Cassandra suggested we go for a walk. She said she had a surprise for me.

I tugged back as we walked through the cemetery gates, but she pulled me along.

The new headstone had been erected with your name on it along with Dad's, and fresh new grass grew where the mound of earth had been.

Cassandra had bedecked it with flowers. I cried. A lot. Strangely enough, I felt better for it.

You loved Hallowe'en, didn't you, Mum?

When I was little you told me and all my friends that you were a witch and they were to look out for you flying past their bedrooms at midnight.

You even had a little witch dangling in your window all year round, which you said was a model of you.

"We're having a Hallowe'en party," Cassandra announced. "Everyone can dress up."

That shook me a bit because you were the one who always made the costumes and put up the fake webs and dangling spiders.

It wasn't the same without you. Nothing is.

Neither Cassandra nor I like fireworks. The noise makes us both jump, but you loved them, so every November we went along to a display with

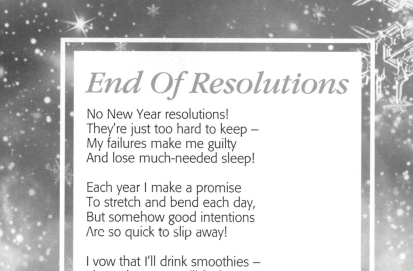

End Of Resolutions

No New Year resolutions!
They're just too hard to keep –
My failures make me guilty
And lose much-needed sleep!

Each year I make a promise
To stretch and bend each day,
But somehow good intentions
Are so quick to slip away!

I vow that I'll drink smoothies –
I know how great I'll feel,
But somehow tea and biscuits
Have so much more appeal!

Instead, what I am planning,
In this I'm quite sincere,
Is just to count my blessings
Each day throughout the year!

Eileen Hay

ear plugs in our ears and fixed, rather tense smiles on our faces.

It seemed wrong to be relieved not to have to go, but Cassandra bought a packet of sparklers and we stood out in the garden whirling them round and giggling.

All these special dates were hard, but Christmas was the worst. I always felt you brought it with you when you came to stay on Christmas Eve, and the house always seemed empty when you'd gone back home after the New Year.

For years it was the three of us and now we are only two. Cassandra was as lost as I was as we opened our presents.

You sitting in the big armchair watching and exclaiming with glee every time we opened something was such a big part of it.

Your enjoyment of our joy somehow made us feel safe and secure.

And every year you'd ask for not too much Christmas dinner and then have seconds.

Then there was the Christmas evening game of Scrabble. You and your naughty words and made-up words and the rules you invented as you went along. You always kept score.

I opened the box and the notebook was still in there, with years of scores written down: our names, *Granny*, *Mum* and *Cassie* underlined in coloured felt-tip.

Cassandra started playing when she was eight and she soon began to match your talent for making up her own words.

We decided we should play a game in your honour. Cassandra made up words and I used a few rude ones.

We ended up laughing and crying, but truth be told, we were both relieved when the day was done.

Last night we sat up to see in the New Year, but we both fell asleep, as always, and you weren't there to shake us awake, so we missed the ships and the fireworks.

*   *   *   *

And now we've come full circle. But I can smell pastries baking, and when I finally get myself downstairs, I think for a moment you've come back.

You're in the kitchen with your long fair hair in a plait, your back towards me as you bob down to take a tray of croissants out of the oven.

But, of course, it's not you. It's Cassandra. She's so like you in more than looks. She turns and smiles.

"Happy New Year, Mum," she says.

How could I have thought I didn't want to get up? We have a whole new year ahead of us. Twelve months to write new stories and to enjoy what life has to offer.

Cassandra will be looking at universities and her blank page will be packed with adventures.

I don't know how I'd have got through this last year without her. I'm so lucky. I put my arms round her and she hugs me back.

There will always be clouds, but my daughter is my sunshine.

"I love you, Cassandra," I say.

"Mu-um!" She giggles. "I love you, too."

I know grief doesn't just stop after a year. All those dates throughout the year will still be hard, but maybe not quite as hard as they were last year.

You always said that time heals eventually.

For the past 12 months, Cassandra has been telling me constantly that Granny wouldn't want us to be sad, and I know she's right.

So this year, every day, on my blank sheet of paper, I'm going to write, *Be happy*.

I realise I have so much to be happy about and such a lot to be grateful for.

You might be gone, Mum, but I know now that you will never leave us. ∎

King's Lynn, Norfolk

One of Britain's major ports in the 12th century, King's Lynn was also a centre for associated industries, such as shipbuilding and rope-making. Later, a glass-making industry developed. Brewing also became important.

Situated on the main trading routes of the Hanseatic League, the merchant association that dominated Northern European maritime trade in the late Middle Ages, Bishop's Lynn, as it had become known, enjoyed great prosperity. Some of the surviving architecture in the town dates back to those times, including the only remaining Hanseatic warehouse in England.

The town has always been popular with visitors. Back in the 18th century, "Robinson Crusoe" author Daniel Defoe described King's Lynn as "beautiful, well built and well situated".

Thanks to international influences on its development, the town has been used as a filming location to represent places in the Netherlands or France, including in the BBC comedy series "'Allo, 'Allo". It's a sought-after setting for British-based productions, too, and fans of the 1980s "Sherlock Holmes" series starring Jeremy Brett, or of the BBC's "Lovejoy", will find many settings familiar.

Who Needs Roses?

by Vivien Brown

I'M not really much of a romantic. I suppose that comes from being married to Alan for so long. He was never one for big romantic gestures – or small ones, either, come to think of it.

Oh, he loved me, all right, or I thought he did, but he had his own way of showing it.

He'd make me a cup of tea and bring it up to bed first thing, kissing me on the forehead before he went to work, or he'd buy me a new pair of gardening gloves when the last ones got a bit threadbare.

Those are the things I've missed the most, the little everyday things that just go with having a man around the house.

Not the bunches of roses and boxes of chocolates, which were never really his style; and to be honest, there's nothing to stop me buying those myself, is there?

But that kiss every morning, and that cuppa I didn't have to make for myself, well, they were special.

He might not have been good at presents, but he never forgot my birthday, although I did make sure I always dropped enough hints in the weeks before.

He bought me the same perfume every Christmas, too, but only because he knew how much I liked it. But Valentine's Day usually came and went pretty much unnoticed in our house.

Alan was the down-to-earth practical sort who would happily dig the garden, mow the lawn or put up a shelf, but he couldn't tell a lily from lavender, and as for all those shiny red Valentine's balloons . . . he'd have said balloons were meant for pinning up at parties, and even then only really for kids.

The shops are full of it right now, of course. The card shops, the supermarkets, the florists. They all overflowing with little fluffy teddies, mugs with *I Love You* scrawled all over them, special bouquets tied with red ribbons, and row upon row of cards covered in hearts and filled with

Illustration by iStock.

mushy poems and words of undying love.

Love isn't undying, though, is it? It certainly died for Alan, which is why he left me for a girl he met at work. Ten years younger than me, quite a lot prettier, and now the mother of his child . . . when we'd decided, together, that children probably weren't for us.

I try not to feel bitter about it, but I can't help wondering if he takes her tea and kisses her every morning, too. Still, with a young baby in their small flat, she's probably awake and out of bed before he is.

"Look what I found," my friend Annie said earlier today, coming back into the office after lunch with a paper bag from which she produced a cactus with a tiny red velvet heart wrapped in its prickly arms. "Ouch!"

"Prickles get you?"

She nodded, sucking at the little dot of blood coming from the end of her thumb.

"My own fault. I should have been more careful. But don't you think it's sweet?

"It would feel a bit funny buying Jason flowers, but this is the perfect alternative. And he can be a prickly devil, so it just seemed apt, somehow."

"Well, if we're after suitable gifts, I'll have to get Steve the biggest balloon I can find, as he's always so full of hot air!" Jean chipped in, and we all laughed. "What about you, Laura? Got your eye on anything special for Valentine's?"

15

I snorted.

"Well, a man would be a good start!"

"How about Mr Robinson?" Jean whispered a bit too loudly for comfort. "He's single, isn't he?"

I gazed towards our boss's office, making sure the door was shut so he wouldn't hear.

"Matchmaking again? I've told you, I'm fine on my own."

"I'm sure he has a soft spot for you, and since your Alan did a runner, this is the first year you've been free."

"Don't remind me. I'll be glad when today's been and gone. All this romance is starting to get me down."

"Only because you don't have any of your own."

"I can't miss what I never had, Jean."

"Nonsense. Just because your Alan never bought you roses doesn't mean —"

"Oh, stop it. Let's get back to work or Mr Robinson will be giving us our cards, and I don't mean pink ones with hearts on!"

The afternoon passed slowly, and my mind kept wandering back to what Jean had said. She was right, of course. Our boss did have a soft spot for me. Well, he did once.

In fact, I had to admit that many years ago, when we had been at school together, it had been mutual, him the good-looking star of the football team and me the chubby one with glasses who was constantly surprised by his attention.

But Sam Robinson and I were destined not to be. He had disappeared off to university hundreds of miles away and I had met Alan and married young.

It had been a shock to discover, six months after I came to work here, that he was to be my new boss. He was transferring from another branch, having moved back following his divorce, and of course we recognised each other instantly, but we kept our history to ourselves.

It didn't feel like a good idea to let the rest of the staff know we had once been so close. Jealousy and rumours of favouritism can so often rear their ugly heads, so we simply kept our mouths shut and told no-one.

That was almost two years ago now. We have little chats sometimes, when nobody else is about, remembering the old days, and he was suitably sympathetic when he heard about Alan leaving, but that's all.

I've never even asked about his ex-wife and the two children whose photos stand in frames on his desk. I know how much a break-up can hurt and I figure that, when and if he wants to tell me, he will.

*　*　*　*

It was cold driving home in the dark, with a sense of impending snow in the air as I hurried inside to pull the curtains shut.

My little tabby cat, Flora, wound herself around my ankles, miaowing for food, which I hastily supplied, and then I was glad to slip my dressing-gown and slippers on and heat up a bowl of soup, eating it in front of the TV with Flora purring on my lap.

Sometimes it didn't seem worth cooking a proper meal when it was just me, and I hardly ever bothered with desserts any more. At least losing a husband had helped me lose a few pounds, too!

Valentine's Day really was everywhere. Adverts for rose bouquets and champagne and special meal-for-two deals . . . Wasn't it a bit late for all that? Surely, by six o'clock in the evening on Valentine's Day itself, everyone would have already bought their flowers and food, wouldn't they?

But then I thought of Alan, and no doubt the countless others just like him, dashing into the local garage or late-night supermarket to scoop up a last-minute card or a cheap bottle of plonk, and it didn't seem quite so unlikely after all.

The whole thing was becoming as commercial as Christmas, if not more so. And they called it romance! Still, after tonight it would all be over for another year, and life could go back to its normal humdrum self.

The ring at the doorbell made me jump. Flora leapt off my lap and hid behind the sofa as I peered out through the curtains.

I didn't usually get visitors in the evenings and wasn't exactly looking my best in my pale pink dressing gown, which I could now see had two fresh blobs of spilt tomato soup down its front.

In the dim light from the porch, where two of the three bulbs had blown and I hadn't got around to replacing them, I could see a man, standing with his back to me, and holding a bunch of roses.

It was Sam Robinson! He must have seen the curtain twitch as he turned and waved, stamping his feet on the step to keep them warm, and I had no option but to go and let him in.

"Hello, Laura, I hope you don't mind . . . but it's so hard to talk privately at the office."

"It's fine. It's not as if I was going anywhere. You'll have to excuse the outfit." I gestured towards my stained gown and laughed.

"Oh, I've seen you in worse. Hockey kit covered in mud, grass stains on your tennis skirt, and that day you spilled milk all over yourself in my mum's kitchen. Remember that?"

"I think you'll find it was you who spilled that milk. I just happened to be the poor soul who got in its way."

"Oh, yes, you could be right!"

He followed me down the hall and into the kitchen.

"Tea?"

"Love one. And these are for you, obviously." He thrust the roses into my hand, looking a bit sheepish, as I flipped the kettle on.

"Really? Why?"

"Does there have to be a reason? But as you want one . . . we're old friends. I'm sorry that I never get the chance to talk to you properly at work, and my mum always taught me to take a gift when I go courting. So that's three!"

"Courting?"

"Sorry, did I say courting? I meant visiting. As if you'd be interested in going out with me!" There was a glint in his eyes, and I could tell he was on the verge of laughing.

"Stop winding me up, Sam Robinson. It's Valentine's Day and you've come carrying roses. You're in danger of me taking you seriously, and then where would you be?"

"Ah, but the roses are white, not red."

"I can see that. But I like white roses. I prefer them, in fact. Less predictable, less . . . corny."

"I know. I remember."

"Do you now?" I poured two mugs of tea and added a spoon of sugar to Sam's without having to ask. "See? I remember things, too."

"Laura? Can we talk? I mean, properly talk. About the important stuff. Your husband, my wife . . ."

"Both exes now."

"Yes, they are. Which means, I hope, that we're both free to move on. Ready to move on . . ."

We sat side by side on my sofa, Flora emerging and pouncing straight on to Sam's lap, which was a positive sign. Cats know a good person when they see one.

"I always liked you."

"I know. I always liked you, too. But I was never really good enough, was I? And you had your big plans. Moving away, uni, a career. I knew I didn't figure in any of that."

"You could have done."

"You wouldn't have wanted me. I was overweight and I wore glasses and . . ."

Sam frowned.

"Why do you always put yourself down, Laura? Beauty is something that comes from within, that shines out of a person.

"And you had plenty of that. We got on so well, didn't we? We talked a lot, we laughed a lot, but I didn't want to tie you down, not when I was going away for three years. I suppose I always hoped that you'd still be here, waiting for me, when I came home from uni.

"When I heard you'd married Alan, I steered clear, but –"

"Don't, Sam. Please."

"Why? Your marriage failed, and so did mine. And the more I see you, the more I want to put things right. Start where we left off. Try again."

I looked at him suspiciously.

"You heard the girls talking today, didn't you?"

"I don't know what you mean."

"Oh, yes, you do. Even after all these years I can read you like a book. Jean and Annie and their matchmaking!

"You realised I'm a sad singleton with nobody to share my Valentine's Day and you decided to come round here and bring me roses.

"I'm perfectly OK on my own, as you will have heard me tell the girls if you had listened long enough."

Sam smiled.

"I don't know what you're talking about. I really don't. But as you may have noticed, I, too, am a sad singleton these days, so I wondered if maybe we could spend the evening together. Eat, drink, be merry . . ."

"Everywhere will be booked up." I knew I was being difficult. "And I've already had some soup."

Sam's eyes twinkled.

"So I see."

We settled into silence, the TV still flickering in front of us.

"Don't you want any food, then? I'm starving."

He put his hand into the carrier bag he'd brought in and started to draw things out. A bottle of red wine, two creamy desserts, some kind of ready meal for two, a packet of pre-sliced green beans and a box of hazelnut truffles.

"A supermarket meal-for-two deal?" I laughed, imagining him rushing round the aisles on his way here, picking up the roses as he went.

Did he really remember I preferred white or were they all that were left in the shop?

Sam glared at me.

"Nothing wrong with that. And if you say no, I'll slink back home with my tail between my legs and eat the lot. But you're not saying no, are you?"

"Maybe to the dessert. I hardly ever eat them these days. I have to watch my figure."

"You know what I'm going to say, don't you?"

"It's a figure worth watching?"

"Exactly. The old ones are still the best.

"Now, lead me to your microwave and a corkscrew, and let's get this party started."

"Can I go up and get changed?"

Sam turned and looked me up and down.

"I rather fancy you just the way you are."

I couldn't help laughing.

"You old flatterer, you!"

I went upstairs and stood for a moment in front of the mirror in my bedroom. Was Sam right? Was I ready to start again? With him?

* * * *

"Before we go any further," he said later, as we stood side by side and washed up the plates, "I have to tell you I have children."

"I know you do. I've seen the photos."

"And is that going to be a problem? You and Alan never . . .?"

"No, we didn't have children. Alan and I didn't do a lot of things, but that's not to say I'm not open to new experiences now."

He glanced at me sideways.

"And to new love?"

I finally allowed myself to slip into his open arms.

"I think you'll find this is not so new. I prefer to call it an old love rediscovered. Happy Valentine's Day, Sam." ■

Bye, Bye, Blackbird

by Kate Finnemore

I HEAR my son Archie approaching way before he comes running into the kitchen.

"Mum, it's Fluffball. I've seen him. He's back!"

"Fluffball's come back? Hey, there, mind the iron," I say as he slams into my side. "It's hot."

Archie has just turned five and will be starting school in a couple of weeks' time, so I'm ironing the creases out of the shirts and trousers we bought yesterday.

"You were wrong, Mum. Fluffball's OK. Come and see." Archie is grinning hugely and bouncing up and down with excitement. "Come on, let's go!"

He tugs at my hand and I laugh, reaching back quickly to switch the iron off before allowing myself to be led through to the lounge.

Archie has pushed a chair over to the window that looks out across the back garden.

Letting go of my hand, he races over and scrambles up on to it, rocking it for an instant on to two legs. I draw in a sharp breath and wince.

"Careful," I warn, crossing the room to stand beside him.

"He was on the grass!" Archie wails in disappointment. "He's not there now."

I hear the sadness in his voice and see it in his face, and my heart aches with love for him.

I pull him into a hug which he promptly squirms out of, leaning forward and resting his hands on the window-sill.

Mark says I'm over-protective.

"You worry too much, Ella," he says. Sometimes I can hear the exasperation in his tone. "You must learn to let him go."

He thinks I'll turn Archie into an overly cautious mother's boy. But he's our only child and I can't help wanting to cocoon him and shield him

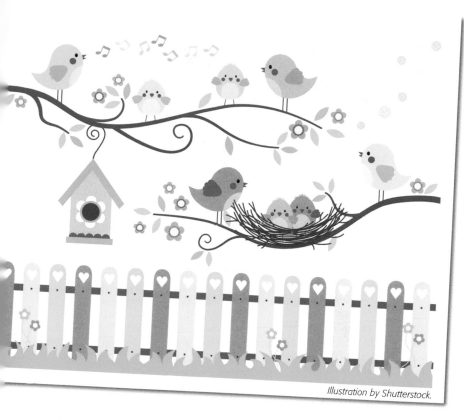

from life's knocks.

I touch my knuckles to my son's cheek.

"Let's just stay here a while, then, sweetie," I say softly. "See if he comes back."

The blackbirds had built their nest in the rose bush that climbed up the back wall of the house.

Archie had been playing in his sandpit one day a few weeks before when he heard the sudden rustle of leaves and flap of wings, and he'd come running in to tell me.

From then on, we'd often stand or sit in the garden, watching from a distance while the female sat on her eggs and the male brought her grubs and bugs.

"Yuk, it's still wriggling," Archie would say, eyeing what the bird held in its beak with gleeful fascination.

Several days later, we heard tiny chirpings and knew the eggs had hatched.

Soon, both adult birds were bringing food to the nest, a constant relay, beaks crammed with fat white grubs, winged insects or long brown worms.

Archie loved it. I held him up so he could see the chicks, two of them, feathers fluffed out, now filling the nest.

Often, if we got too close, one of the adults would swoop low past us while the other hopped combatively along a metre length of the fence, making a harsh sound like a dry twig snapping, and I'd pull Archie back.

One morning, I found one of the chicks lying dead on the ground beneath the nest. I buried it in a corner of the garden before Archie could see it.

"You should have left it," Mark said. "He needs to learn life can be cruel at times. Nature red in tooth and claw, and all that."

"No." My response was instinctive.

But as I watched Mark cycle down the road to work, I wondered if maybe he was right. Archie had to learn some time, and it wasn't as if the chick was a much-loved pet.

Then the second chick fledged.

"He's like a little ball of fluff," Archie said, breathless with excitement.

"Then we'll call him Fluffball."

The chick was on the ground, partially hidden, close to where stems of honeysuckle came out of the soil.

He stood so still, and the speckled golds and browns of his plumage were such a perfect match with his surroundings, that it would have been easy to miss him.

It was only when, finally, Fluffball moved out from behind the honeysuckle that I saw something was very wrong. I must have made a sound because Archie twisted round to look at me.

"What is it?"

"His right leg's trailing behind him. If he can't walk properly, he, um —" I cleared my throat. "He might not survive, Archie."

*　*　*　*

Now, it's three days later, and Archie reckons he's seen him and that he has survived, and that's great news.

Standing next to my son, one arm resting across his shoulders, I watch eagerly out of the window and offer up a silent prayer that he's right.

And there he is — unmistakable as he hops across the grass. My heart leaps in relief. Not only is Fluffball still alive, but his right leg seems to be trailing much less. I begin to believe that he might have a chance, after all.

I look around for the parents, and catch sight of the female, not on the roof of our garage but further away, on next door's roof.

There are no worms in her beak and it occurs to me that, though she's keeping an eye on her chick from a distance, she's letting him find out about the world by himself.

I realise the blackbird's got the right idea. She's still there for Fluffball, but she's letting him go, giving him the space to find his own way. And I must do the same.

My hand slides from my son's shoulders and I step back a pace.

"He'll be all right," I whisper. "And so will you." ■

Shutterstock.

Highclere Castle

Cue the music, and the grand building that sweeps into view transports us to the lives of the upstairs-downstairs creations of Julian Fellowes and his much-loved "Downton Abbey". However, Highclere Castle in Hampshire – the "real" Downton – is home to the 8th Earl and Countess of Carnarvon, who look after the 300 or so rooms set within 1,000 acres of grounds designed by none other than landscape architect Lancelot "Capability" Brown.

Highclere has been with the Carnarvon family since 1842, and the grand building we see today was remodelled by Sir Charles Barry, who also designed the Houses of Parliament. A more palatial family home would be difficult to find; however, this one has a particularly interesting asset tucked away in the cellars.

Think back to the 5th Earl of Carnarvon, the gentleman who funded the search for the burial site of Tutankhamun, and that gives a clue to some of the artefacts and replicas of treasures to be found in this Grade-I-listed building. It was back in 1922 that the world watched in wonder as Howard Carter literally struck gold on his final mission to find the tomb of the boy pharaoh.

Not Just For Birthdays

by Valerie Bowes

M ANDY'S brow creased in uncertainty.
At last she'd thought of the perfect thing to give Luke for his birthday, only to find she'd left it too late. Now she wouldn't be able to get one until after the eagerly awaited day.

Well, she could – possibly – if she hunted around, but it wouldn't be one of the ones she wanted. One of the ones he wanted.

So what was she going to do?

Precious time went past while Mandy tried to force her brain into thinking of a solution, but no lightbulb moment illuminated the way. Then, walking past a charity shop, she saw the answer.

The item in the window wasn't exactly what she had in mind, but it gave her an idea.

She wasn't sure if she could do it, but she could picture Luke's face when he opened the parcel and realised what she'd got him, and it brought a smile to her own.

For now, she had to find the necessary bits and pieces to make a start.

It wasn't easy. She couldn't find a pattern, so she had to get something as similar as possible and trust she could alter it to suit.

And it would be hard. It wasn't a thing she'd done since Luke was a grainy picture on a scan.

Steve had laughed at her efforts back then.

"What's that supposed to be?"

She held up the tiny garment.

"What does it look like? It's a little jacket, of course."

"Honestly, Mandy. Babies don't wear that sort of thing nowadays, even if it looked even vaguely like a jacket. Which it doesn't."

She'd reddened.

"It will when it's finished. And it'll be made with love."

"Ditch it, Mand. We'll buy stuff like everybody else."

"It's only for his first things," she said, concealing the hurt. "He'll have all the cool trackie bottoms and tops with dinosaurs on when he's big enough to know what he's wearing."

She tried to explain that she needed to do this. That she wanted the first things that nestled next to her son's skin to be made by her, not some anonymous factory worker, but he didn't understand.

The marriage lasted until Luke was three years old.

*   *   *   *

Mandy hadn't been a proficient knitter even 13 years ago. But now she bought the wool and the needles, waited until Luke had gone up to his room with strict instructions not to spend more than half an hour on his computer, and cast on the first stitch.

She had to unpick more than once, but gradually it took shape. She stuffed it carefully and tied a big red bow around its neck to stop its head from wobbling.

Then she packed it carefully into a gaily wrapped box and put it on the table with his card, picturing his excitement.

She kept the box until last, when all the other presents had been opened and exclaimed over.

Normally she couldn't compete with Steve's present – expensive, and usually a computer game or something that caused problems when she restricted its use.

25

But, this time, she thought she'd hit the jackpot.

Luke tore off the paper, grinning in anticipation, and opened the box. She'd been prepared for some smart comment, like, "Did you get me mixed up with Liam?"

Luke's small cousin still wouldn't go to bed without floppy-eared Blue Rabbit.

She'd been expecting puzzled laughter and raised eyebrows.

What she hadn't expected was that Luke would flush a furious scarlet and hurl the box across the room, while his eyes filled with tears.

"You think this is funny?"

"Luke . . ." she began, but he wasn't listening.

"Dad always says you think homemade things are worth more than things you buy, but I'm not a baby now, Mum!"

He smeared the angry tears from his cheeks and ran from the room.

First Crush

It's hard to love somebody when you have to join the queue,
When the object of your passion is beloved by others, too.
When you want his sole attention, but you're standing in a crowd,
And though you call his name out, all the rest scream just as loud.
It's hard when he's performing, singing songs of love so true.
Did he really get your letter? Are his words meant just for you?
He seems to smile straight at you, and your heart is beating fast –
But no! The gig is over. He is gone, and you're aghast.
It's hard to love a pop star, when you're very young and green,
Which gives me some small comfort now I'm long past sweet
    sixteen!

Maggie Ingall

Mandy heard the front door open and shut.

She ran after him, seeing him tearing down the road, but she was only wearing socks and the road was wet.

He turned the corner and, by the time she got there, he had disappeared.

Slithering back as fast as she could, Mandy crammed her feet into some shoes, searched frantically for her car keys and raced outside.

She reversed out of the drive and set off down the road. But as soon as she turned the corner, he was there. He was heading homewards, his hands thrust deep in his pockets and his head bowed, his wet hair flopping into his face.

He looked up as she brought the car to a stop and leaned over to open the door. He got in without a word, but she'd seen that his eyes were still full of tears.

Not a thing was said until they were once more in the warm sitting-room with its cheerful birthday banner.

"Sorry, Mum. It's just that . . . it's not that I'm disappointed or anything . . . it's just that I really, really want . . ."

"Come here."

Mandy pulled him into her arms, resting her head on top of his with a tiny portion of her brain registering that it wouldn't be long before he was too tall for her to do that.

She'd so hoped that Steve's belief that he could buy his way into his son's affections had been fruitless. And she knew Luke hadn't inherited that side of his father's character.

With a last squeeze, she let him go. He bent to pick up the knitted dog.

"Did you think I was Liam or something?"

She almost laughed, but held it in until he'd discovered why she'd given it to him.

"Why don't you read the card?" she suggested, nodding towards where it still lay unopened.

He pulled it from its envelope and his eyes grew big with wonder. A smile spread itself over his lips as he read the words a second time, this time aloud.

The puppy that's waiting for you looks a bit like this and he'll be ready to leave his mum at the end of the month.

"A dog? A real, live one?"

Mandy nodded.

"Only if you promise to look after it, mind. A dog isn't just for Christmas. Or birthdays."

He hugged her again, so hard she thought a rib might crack.

"Of course I will. It's what I'd hoped for, that's why I freaked when I thought you'd made me a toy instead. It'll be good training for when I become a vet, won't it?

"Wow! A dog!"

He looked at her carefully knitted replica, with the white coat, dark brown patch over one eye and long, whip-like tail.

"One of Bella's puppies? Cool!"

"I couldn't find a knitting pattern that looked exactly like him, so I sort of made it up," Mandy explained.

"Can I see?"

She took the pattern from its hiding-place and showed him. He grinned.

"Good job, Ma! Though I can see where you might need a little practice!"

She pretended to thump him, but he was still staring at the pattern.

"And that's it!" he said, pointing to the logo printed across the top. "That's the perfect name for him."

"Hobby Create?"

He held the toy dog close to his heart.

"Mum, meet Hob." ■

Mermaid Quay, Cardiff

The waterfront of Cardiff Bay and Mermaid Quay is a familiar sight thanks to its frequent appearance in the BBC's "Doctor Who", which is produced in Cardiff. Before the construction of the Cardiff Bay Barrage in 1999, though, the bay was tidal, revealing vast mud flats at low tide. The conversion created a new freshwater lake, and Mermaid Quay, part of the new development, opened in 1999.

One of Cardiff's most famous landmarks is the Grade-I-listed Pierhead Building, featuring a distinctive clock so similar to Big Ben that it's known as "baby Big Ben". Built in 1897 as the headquarters of the Bute Dock Company, the building later became the headquarters of the Cardiff Railway Company, then the offices of the Port of Cardiff.

It was opened as a visitor attraction for the Welsh Parliament in 2010 and the building is now an important visitor, events and conference venue for the people of Wales.

So Shall I Sew

by Laura Tapper

"THERE, thank goodness that's done."

Madeline Hartman lifted the shiny silver foot on the machine and drew her work around to the back, where a concealed blade sliced neatly through the threads.

She loved running her own little sewing business, but when Mrs White had walked in with four pairs of trousers, three skirts and six dresses to be taken up in time for her last-minute holiday, Madeline's heart had sunk.

Although alterations were her bread-and-butter work, they could get rather tedious and she much preferred to intersperse them with more creative jobs. It felt good to have got them out of the way.

As she was folding up all the items, ready for collection, she took a moment to glance out of the window.

There he was again. Three days in a row, she had seen a man hanging around on the street outside at lunchtime, peering in.

It was definitely the same guy because he was quite distinctive: well over six feet tall and clearly a gym member, judging by the wide shoulders and slim hips.

On each of the previous days he'd walked away, so out of sheer curiosity, Madeline decided to go out and speak to him.

"Good morning. Do you need any help?" She gave him a friendly smile from the doorway of her little shop.

The man immediately started, as though he'd been caught in the act of something suspicious.

"Oh, I'm not sure. Is this place just for women? There seem to be a lot of dresses and girlie things in the windows."

"No, no, I'll happily sew for anybody, as long as they pay me." Madeline laughed, and opened the door wider. "Come in and tell me what you need."

After a moment's hesitation, he followed her inside and stood in the

Illustration by Sarah Holliday.

middle of the floor, staring around at the walls with a bewildered expression.

They were covered with patterns, ribbons, buttons, threads and haberdashery of all kinds. In the centre of one wall, there was a traditional, Victorian-style cross-stitched sampler bearing the same legend as the hand-painted sign on the shop front: *As you rip, so shall I sew.*

He pointed to it.

"Does that mean you only do repairs?"

Madeline carried on putting the last of Mrs White's items in the large bag as she replied.

"Not at all. Alterations are my most regular jobs and I do a lot of curtains, but I make things up from scratch, too. I specialise in bespoke dresses for occasions like school proms and weddings."

Her hands became still and her expression slightly dreamy.

"And I made all the costumes for a local dance troupe taking part in a festival. Forty little tap-dancing undersea creatures aged between four and eleven was no mean feat, I can tell you!"

She set the bag on the floor, smoothed the front of her calico cross-back apron and came to stand in front of him.

"So what I'm saying is, anything you want, from a specific colour of shirt for a wedding to a Minion costume for a fancy-dress party, I'll do my best to achieve it for you."

His brow furrowed.

"Why bother with the sign, then? Isn't it a bit misleading?"

Madeline walked over to the sampler and stroked the old-fashioned wooden frame.

"My great-great-grandfather was a tailor and his wife stitched this to hang in his shop over a century ago.

"It's been handed down through the family ever since, but mostly stayed in a box in the loft because nobody else had any interest in sewing, until I came along."

She spread her arms wide.

"When I decided to open this place, my grandma remembered it and dug it out. I hadn't named the shop then, and that decided it: So Shall I Sew."

The man seemed to consider that for a moment and then shrugged.

"Makes sense, I guess. He'd probably be pretty chuffed to know that someone in his family finally took after him."

"I like to think so." Madeline nodded and picked up her order book and pencil. "Now, to business – what is it that you need help with?"

Straight away, his cheeks filled with colour and he bit at his lip.

"It's a bit awkward. I'm not sure how to explain it."

"Look, no matter what it is, you can trust me to be absolutely discreet. Whatever is said in here is in complete confidence and would never be revealed to anyone." Her tone was gentle and her expression earnest.

"Plus, I'm pretty unshockable – believe me, you have to be in this business."

His dark brown eyes held her grey ones for a few moments. He seemed to be weighing up the truth of her words and then she could see his expression change as he came to a decision.

"OK, well, the truth is that I have a problem with my clothes because, no matter what size I buy, they never fit me properly and they never will, because I'm just too big."

Madeline looked him up and down, totally confused.

"But you're in great shape, if you don't mind me saying. You clearly look after yourself. Most guys would give their eye-teeth to have your build!"

"Oh, I know I'm fit." As soon as the words were out of his mouth, his eyes flicked away from hers and his cheeks got even redder. "I mean . . . I go to the gym a lot and I work really hard to keep in trim . . ."

Madeline's laugh rang out.

"You don't have to apologise for knowing you're fit – trust me, you are. The closest I get to vigorous exercise is a bit of running stitch, so I take my hat off to you, but I think I can guess what the issue might be." Her voice became soft and encouraging.

"Purely in my professional capacity, can I ask you to remove your jacket, so I can take a look?"

Without lifting his gaze from the carpet, he unzipped the loose waterproof jacket he was wearing to reveal a classic formal shirt in a light sky blue, which he'd coupled with a silk tie bearing what was an attractively modern take on paisley.

He was clearly a man with an eye for colour and pattern. It all looked fantastic on him until her gaze reached his arms and shoulders.

There, the fabric was straining at the seams and it was a wonder the shirt was holding together at all. In fact, she couldn't imagine how he'd managed to get the garment on.

"See what I mean?" He held out his hands close to his thighs and she saw that he had a similar issue with his trousers. "Is this something you can deal with?"

Madeline took a deep breath.

"Absolutely. No job is too small, or too big." She pulled out a chair for him to sit down by her consultation table. "I've got a range of options we can talk through and then it will all get sorted.

"My name's Madeline." She held out her hand and he took it, looking relieved.

"I'm Richard and I'm so pleased to meet you. Thank you."

They spent the next ten minutes talking through the choices Madeline had to offer to get clothes that would fit Richard's body shape.

They came to the conclusion that he would be better, at least in the beginning, to buy ready-made items in larger sizes, which Madeline could then tailor to fit.

Later on, he could always choose to have bespoke items made, but that would come at a much higher cost. Madeline was interested in how he had coped with the issue up until then.

Richard explained that he had always been keen on fitness and had previously been a personal trainer.

Recently, he'd made the big decision to change career and had gone into office work instead, which had caused the problem with his clothes.

"All these muscles look fine in sweatpants and vests, but they don't work so well in formal shirts and trousers."

"What made you switch jobs, if you enjoy the gym so much? I would have thought personal training was the dream role for you."

Having made a note of all the details she needed for the moment, Madeline closed her order book.

"Personally, I love the fact that I can make a living out of what would be my hobby anyway."

"That's what I thought – and it was fun to begin with – but it's not like running a shop.

"The hours are so antisocial that it's hard to have any friends or fun outside of work, and your customers don't come to you, so you're always chasing the business, travelling here, there and everywhere.

"Plus it's pretty unreliable because, when money's a bit tight, the personal trainer is the first thing to go. Trust me – nobody wants to spend time in the gym in December." He gave a wry grin. "Apart from me, that is."

"Wow, that's all so different from what I do. This is very steady, mostly, but coming up to Christmas it's like a madhouse in here, with commissioned gifts, party dresses, new curtains ready for family coming to stay – it gets a bit crazy.

"The rest of the year it's a straight nine to four, although I do open Saturday mornings."

Richard glanced at his watch, stood up from the table and put his jacket back on.

"I'd better be getting back to work. Thank you so much for your time, Madeline. I'm really glad you spotted me through the window, or I might still be walking up and down dithering."

Madeline went with him to the door.

"Oh, you don't give yourself enough credit. This place must be way out of your comfort zone, and you did far better than I would have done if I'd had to walk into a leisure centre full of mirrors and Lycra-coated gym-bunnies.

"Besides, it's been a pleasure meeting you. Come back when you have the things you want to be altered and I'll take it from there."

She watched as Richard crossed the road and walked up the street towards the commercial part of the city. Catching a glimpse of her own reflection in the window, she sighed.

Much as she might make jokes about it, Madeline had never been happy with what she saw in the mirror.

It wasn't quite true that she didn't exercise – she did plenty of walking and she enjoyed a swim, but she had never felt comfortable in a gym.

And it was the fact that the fashion industry didn't really cater for the shorter, rounder figure that had created her interest in dressmaking in the first place.

It was so weird to think that someone like Richard, who could be a poster boy for the fitness industry, could lack confidence in any way.

Well, Madeline knew better than anyone how great it felt to finally have clothes that fitted, and it was her job to spread that joy around.

*　　*　　*　　*

"It's gorgeous. She's going to love it. I can't believe how well it's turned out." The lady ran her hands over the quilt laid out on the sewing table.

"The way you've put all the different fabrics together and used the buttons and ribbons for decoration. You're so clever."

"I'm just glad it's matched your expectations." Madeline began gently folding it up. "I was quite nervous because, if you didn't like it, there was no going back."

"Well, I don't think you had anything to worry about. This has been worth every penny and I'll be recommending you to all my friends. It's the perfect way to store all those memories."

They went over to the counter at the back of the shop to put the payment through the card machine and then the woman left, clutching the quilt close to her as though it were the most precious thing in the world.

"Sorry to keep you waiting – I know you're on your lunch break."

Richard was sitting quietly at the consultation desk.

"That's OK, I'm in no hurry. That looked like a complicated piece of work. What was it all about?"

"Oh, that was a memory quilt. One of my favourite things to do, but always really nerve-racking because it involves cutting up things that can't be replaced."

Richard frowned and shook his head.

"What on earth do you mean?"

"Well, that quilt was made out of the clothes which were worn by that lady's three grandchildren when they were little. I chopped them up, used the fabrics to make the quilt, the buttons and trimmings for embellishment and hand embroidery to add their names and other details. Now their mum will have a permanent memento of their baby years which she can treasure for ever."

"Wow – that's such a great thing to be able to do for someone. No wonder she was so grateful."

Madeline shrugged uncomfortably.

"It's all part of the job. You must have had the same thing when clients were pleased with the way their fitness improved under your guidance."

Richard let out a laugh. It was the first of his that Madeline had heard, rich and deep, coming up from his toned belly to fill the little shop. She immediately caught the infection and joined in.

"Oh, I get it – they weren't thanking you much when you were standing over them pushing them to work harder, sweat more and go for the burn."

Richard nodded.

"Everybody wants their money's worth out of a personal trainer and yet they kind of hate you while you're making sure they get it.

"Some days, clients would rather have gone for a quick trip to the dentist than spend an hour with me." He opened the bag on his knee and took out three shirts.

"I got these at the weekend, so I was hoping you would be able to work some magic on them."

"Sure." Madeline gestured towards a heavy brocade curtain hanging in the corner of the shop. "The changing room is over there.

"If it's OK with you, I think it will help for you to pop one on so I can mark it with pins – although I may have to stand on a box to do it. That way, you'll definitely get the fit you're looking for."

Fifteen minutes later, Richard set off back to the office, agreeing to return in two days' time to try the first shirt. Once again, Madeline found herself following his progress across the road.

A dentist would have to be extremely good looking to be a more appealing option than spending an hour with Richard, no matter how tough a personal trainer he was.

*   *   *   *

"This is perfect." Richard stood in front of the mirror and turned one way and then the other so he could examine the fit of the shirt from all angles. "It's like it was made for me."

He reached forward and then lifted his arms up over his head.

"I can move without feeling like I'm going to split something." His eyes shone as they met Madeline's. "You have no idea what it's like never to be able to find clothes that fit. I felt like a freak."

Suddenly, Madeline's throat tightened and her eyes began to burn.

"I understand better than you might think, but I know everyone is special and unique. That's what my shop is all about." Her voice was almost a whisper.

"It shows in all your work and it's why I've got another job I want to talk to you about." Richard smoothed the crisp white shirt down over his toned abs.

"I know it sounds silly — like a child who's just got new shoes — but is it OK if I keep it on?" He gave her a sheepish grin.

"That's fine." She smiled, her emotions back under control. "I don't blame you. Now we know that one's right, I'll get on with the others."

She took his old shirt from his hand, feeling the warmth from his body still in it, and put it in a bag for him to take away.

"What other project have you got in mind?"

"It's my mother's sixtieth birthday coming up later this year and I wanted to give her something really special." He sat back down at the desk, and she joined him.

"I was talking to my sister about the memory quilt you made for that lady the other day and she suggested we could get you to do a similar thing for Mum. Trouble is, we don't have any old clothes from when we were kids."

"Quilting has a long history and there are lots of ways you can use it to commemorate things and tell stories, even if you use new fabrics.

"I think it's a lovely idea and I'm certain we could come up with something which would make your mum very happy. To start with, you'll need to think about what she might like."

Madeline reached down beside her, lifted up a large wicker basket and placed it on the table. Inside were dozens of folded triangular bundles of fabric in a rainbow of colours and all sorts of patterns.

Richard began to walk through them with his fingers.

"I like this one. It reminds me of our garden at home when we were little, because Mum was always growing strawberries to make jam.

"We'd sneak out and eat them as soon as any got ripe, so she never had enough to cook with." His deep laugh rolled around the room again.

"Put it to one side, then." Madeline glanced at the clock on the wall. "If it were up to me, I'd love you to stay for the afternoon planning this out, but I suspect you've got work to do.

"How about if you come in on Saturday at one o'clock, when I close?" Richard stared at her.

"Would that be OK? Are you sure you don't mind?"

"I'm happy to help on two conditions." Madeline stood up.

"Name them."

"Λ: you need to spend some time thinking about which memories you want to be represented in the quilt, like the strawberries you just mentioned."

"Makes sense." Richard nodded. "What's B?"

"It's your job to bring lunch. Nothing too messy and no prawns." Her nose wrinkled.

"Naturally – there's nothing shellfish about you!" He winked.

Madeline groaned.

"Luckily, I'm fine with a bit of cheese! Now get back to the office to show off that shirt and I'll see you on Saturday."

She stood in the centre of the floor, gazing at his back view through the shop window. Despite the emotional scars school gymnastics lessons had left her with, her stomach seemed happy enough to be doing somersaults down the road after him.

* * * *

"When I was about eight, we all went on holiday to the Isle of Wight. A massive wave caught my mum by surprise and completely knocked her off her feet."

Richard's laugh came more readily now, and Madeline joined him, easily imagining the scene as she hunted through her collection of fat quarters.

"Her glasses fell off, so me and my sister had to dive under the water to find them, before they got washed away."

"How about this?" She shook out a square of fabric with a range of shades of blues in wavy stripes across it.

"We could decorate it, here and there, with some white stitches to create the effect of the foam and I could hand-embroider a pair of specs to complete the story."

Richard's mouth hung open.

"This is the bit I don't get. How can you turn my rambling into an idea like that and immediately know how to present it?"

Madeline shrugged.

"It's just horses for courses." She tugged at the edges of her apron. "If you could see under this, you'd immediately be able to tell me how many crunches and press-ups I ought to do, but we're not going there." She carried the blue material over to the sewing table.

"Now we've collected a few fabrics together, it's time for you to get started."

"Me?" Richard's horror was obvious. "Oh, no – I'm the lunch man. You're in charge of the stitching, surely."

"Well, you've put a lot of thought into this project, but everyone knows that the gifts mums love the most are the ones their kids had a hand in making."

Madeline led him over to the chair behind her sewing machine and used her hands on his muscular back to gently encourage him into it.

"I've got some sample pieces ready for you to practise on first. And don't look so terrified – I'll be with you every step of the way."

For the rest of the afternoon, she guided him through the process of cutting the pieces and stitching them together.

Under her expert and patient tutelage, he learned all about seam allowances, complementary colours, applique, rotary cutters and the importance of pressing his work.

By the end of that session, they were able to stand back and admire his first completed block.

"This tells the story of our childhood perfectly. She was always a fantastic mum. I probably don't thank her enough. Are you sure you don't mind adding the hand embroidery? It feels like this quilt is going to take up a lot of your time."

"Well, you're thanking her now and you needn't worry – I won't be charging by the hour for this one." Madeline was quick to reassure him with a grin.

"You're giving me the chance to let my own creativity run free and I'm loving it. Just come back next Saturday with some more ideas for the next block. Maybe something from your mum's own childhood?"

* * * *

They soon settled into a routine. Every Saturday, Richard would arrive with lunch for them both, along with a head full of memories, which he'd discreetly gathered by chatting with aunts, grandparents and the rest of his family.

While they stitched Richard's mother's stories, they shared their own as well, until it felt as though they'd known each other for years. Finally, the day came when the quilt was finished.

"You've done so much for me, Madeline. Looking at this now, I can hardly believe what we've achieved. I've thought a lot about how I might be able to repay you for sharing your skills with me."

Madeline's chest tightened. She moved away from him to stand facing the long mirror.

His previous job had all been about building the body beautiful and in her head, she'd known it would come down to this in the end, no matter how much her heart had hoped for something else.

"Of course, I'd be grateful for personal training, and goodness knows I probably need it, but I don't really think the gym is for me.

"I'm busy with the shop and I mostly prefer walking . . ." Her voice caught in her throat, trailing off.

Richard came to stand behind her, and she could feel his warmth.

"Everything in this shop is unique, special and perfect because you are, too."

She gasped slightly and looked up, catching his eyes in the mirror. He nodded to her, turning her round so that he could take both her hands in his.

"What I'd like is for you to come with me to my mother's birthday party on Sunday. I want you to see how happy our quilt makes her." He kissed her hands.

"And I want everyone to know how happy you make me – just the way you are." ∎

Shutterstock

Glamis Castle

If walls could talk, this grand residence would have fascinating secrets to reveal, as it is steeped in history spanning centuries. This was the Queen Mother's Scottish childhood home and Princess Margaret's birthplace in 1930. The thanage of Glamis was granted to Sir John Lyon by King Robert II in 1372, and four years later Sir John married the King's daughter, Princess Johanna Stewart.

This majestic building with turrets and towers has been the Lyon family home since the 1400s and remains the residence of Simon Patrick, 19th Earl of Strathmore and Kinghorne.

The oldest part of the building dates from the 15th century, and the 3rd Earl made substantial additions and improvements in the late 17th century.

While Glamis Castle may have been the inspiration behind Shakespeare's "Macbeth", the building has rich tales of ghosts, secret passageways and mysterious bricked-up rooms – little wonder it's regarded as one of Britain's most haunted castles! In fact, the ghostly figure of the "Grey Lady" is said to have a specific seat in the castle's chapel which no-one dares sit in.

Surrounded by acres of beautiful countryside, Glamis Castle was once used as a convalescent hospital to treat injured soldiers in World War I, the healing powers of the landscape aiding recovery. The tree-lined driveway befits such a grand building, which is also home to what is believed to be Scotland's largest sundial.

The Yellow House

by Lynda Franklin

J AYNE saw the yellow house as soon she reached the brow of the hill. The house wasn't really yellow, but the front garden was full to bursting with golden daffodils.

Large, freshly dug beds of yellow shone and shimmered in the spring sunshine and the brick walls of the old house appeared to glow with light.

It was her first walk in the village and she was loving every minute after her hectic life in London.

When she reached the top of the hill, Jayne gazed around her at the view of the countryside and the streets of the village.

When her eye lit on the yellow house, she stopped and stared. It shone like a beacon among the other houses and cottages.

"I wish that house had been for sale when we were looking," she told her husband, Adam, that evening over dinner. "I would have snapped it up."

Adam laughed.

"You don't know how much it's worth."

Jayne shook her head.

"I think I would have paid anything. It just – drew me, you know? I've never seen anything like it."

"Well, that's ridiculous." Adam topped up her glass with non-alcoholic wine. "Good job it wasn't for sale, then. You'd have been selling the dog and the family silver."

He grinned.

"You're pleased with this house, aren't you?"

"Yes, of course I am." Jayne smiled and picked up her glass. "Thanks. I love this cottage; it's perfect for the three of us."

She looked down and gently stroked her hand across her stomach.

"You love your new home, too, don't you?"

They had tried so long for this baby, and now, at forty years old, Jayne

Illustration by Ruth Blair.

was pregnant. It had always been a dream of hers to raise a family in the countryside.

Maybe it was a bit starry-eyed, a bit predictable, but Jayne loved to imagine their child running carefree and barefoot through the grass, exploring the woods and climbing trees, learning about animals and nature and growing up happy and healthy.

There was always sunshine in her dreams, always plenty of laughter and happiness. She took a small sip of her drink, hoping it wouldn't start the heartburn again.

"The garden was so pretty, full of daffodils," she said to Adam.

He looked amused.

"We can plant daffodils, you know."

"I know. You must see it, though, Adam; you'll know what I mean."

Adam snorted.

"I need to finish painting the nursery first. There's enough to do in this house without looking at someone else's."

Jayne laughed softly.

"I know. It's really weird, though. I just sort of suddenly saw it and couldn't stop looking at it."

"Yeah, well," he said gruffly, "you're pregnant, aren't you?"

"What's that supposed to mean?" Jayne asked with a touch of asperity.

"Well, you're sentimental about everything at the moment." Adam continued eating his dinner, worried he had overstepped the mark, but Jayne knew he was right.

The yellow house had made her feel exactly that – sentimental. It was almost as if one of her daydreams had sprung into life, beckoning and pulling her in, and she knew she would walk that way tomorrow.

* * * *

Jayne walked every day now she was no longer working. The countryside surrounding the village was a joy to saunter around, but she always ended up going the same way: down the footpath, across the fields and up to the brow of the hill.

There she would stop, catch her breath, then gaze down at the yellow house. She drank in the garden, the old-fashioned sash windows and solid brick walls.

She loved the greenery growing round the front door and the wonky garden gate. Sometimes she would sit on the grassy hill and do nothing more than stare down into the valley.

There were times she wondered what she was doing, but somehow she couldn't stop. The yellow house was like a magnet, drawing her in.

* * * *

"We ought to sort out the garden a bit, I suppose," Adam said one Saturday. "It's a bit overgrown. The longer we leave it the harder a job it will be."

Jayne nodded.

"As long as the grass is cut it will be all right for a while."

"What about that pond at the end?" Adam pointed down the garden. "Do you want me to buy some fish for it? It's a good-sized one."

Jayne felt an unexpected stab of panic and she looked up sharply.

"No pond. I don't want a pond."

Adam looked at her curiously.

"OK, I'll fill it in. I just thought it would be pretty with some fish in it. Nice in the summer."

Jayne took a deep breath. She still felt rattled, but didn't know where such a strong reaction had come from.

"Sorry – it's just that water's so dangerous for kids."

Adam kissed the top of her head.

"No worries. The pond is gone."

* * * *

The following day Jayne walked up the hill, puffing slightly now the size of her bump was increasing daily.

She'd made sandwiches and a flask of tea, telling herself a relaxing picnic in the meadow would be good for her, especially as the weather was so nice.

She needed to take things easy these last few weeks of pregnancy. She had a couple of magazines and a book about labour that went everywhere with her.

Despite planning to sit in the meadow, Jayne knew exactly where she would end up eating her picnic. Deep down she always knew she would end up on the grassy hill overlooking the yellow house.

Jayne felt the usual surge of pleasure ripple through her as she placed her cardigan on the grass and sat down. There it stood, the pretty yellow house surrounded by a golden hue of flowers.

It seemed to radiate warmth and happiness.

A lady with brown hair speckled with grey was working in the front garden today. She seemed to sense Jayne staring down and she stopped and looked up.

Unsure what to do, Jayne waved. It seemed the most natural thing in the world when the lady waved back.

Jayne packed her sandwiches back into her backpack. It would be so nice to see the yellow house close up, and the lady seemed friendly enough.

She would have to take it slowly, but she decided to walk down the hill and talk to her.

$$* \quad * \quad * \quad *$$

"Hello." Jayne smiled as she reached the wonky gate. "I've just moved in nearby. I hope you don't mind but I just love your house."

The lady looked older now Jayne was face to face with her, but she had a warm, welcoming smile as she nodded.

"I've seen you walking," she said. Her voice had the slightest faint country burr.

"Oh, dear." Jayne laughed. "You must think I'm a stalker!"

The lady smiled.

"Not at all. I see you've got your flask, but would you like to come inside for a fresh cup?"

Jayne had to suppress her excitement at the prospect of going inside the yellow house and she nodded eagerly.

"That's very kind."

The lady was called Lily, and she took Jayne round the side of the house into the garden and through the back door.

The country kitchen was just as Jayne had imagined, and she sat at the wooden table while Lily filled the kettle.

"Let me get the cups for you," Jayne said, jumping up and opening a cupboard door.

Then she stopped, aware of Lily's eyes on her.

"That was a good guess," Lily said.

Jayne felt flummoxed. Why had she done that? There had been no doubt in her mind at all that the cups were in there. How could she possibly have known?

"Yes, I suppose so."

Lily poured the tea and placed a homemade fruitcake on the table, and they chatted about the weather, how different London was from the countryside and, of course, the baby.

"Do you have a family, Lily?" Jayne asked.

Lily nodded.

"A daughter, Bonnie."

"Oh, that's a pretty name."

"Well, she was a bonnie baby, so beautiful it made your heart ache to look at her. Into everything, of course —"

"I daresay she's outgrown that by now," Jayne said with a grin.

Lliy smiled.

"I expect she's keeping heaven on its toes."

Jayne drew in her breath sharply.

"Oh, Lily, I'm so sorry." She reached out and took hold of Lily's hand. It felt comfortable and warm in hers.

Lily gave a small shrug.

"A mother is supposed to keep her child safe. I should have got rid of it."

Jayne kept hold of her hand and didn't say anything, but she felt her

A Picture Of Spring

The clocks move forward
As swallows arrive,
And the world all about us
Comes quickly alive.
Flower buds are bursting
With the sun's stretching rays,
Whilst birds sing in praise of
These warm, longer days.

Spring is a season
And a feeling as well,
Bringing new hope
With its own magic spell.
It's the year's busy time,
When life's resurrected
As God adds the colours
To what he's perfected.

John Darley

heartbeat quicken.

"We filled it in afterwards, of course," Lily was saying. "It wasn't very deep. I never thought anyone could drown in it.

"But a child can drown in a couple of inches, you know. It was terrible – terrible." She gently moved her hand away and forced a smile back on her face.

"Goodness me! Why am I telling you all this? And you about to have a child, as well!"

There was a large photograph on the shelf of a little girl with blonde curls, blue eyes and a face full of smiling curiosity and mischief.

"That's Bonnie," Lily said, seeing Jayne glance at it.

"It was taken on her fourth birthday. She died two days later on the seventh of August, 1979, at two p.m.

"Yes, I know the exact time," she added with a sad smile.

"I went to call her in from the garden, you see. Her favourite programme was coming on. 'Jamie And The Magic Torch', I think it was called. She loved it."

"That's my birthday," Jayne murmured softly. "August the seventh, 1979. I popped into the world at just gone two; in time for dinner, my dad always says."

The two women looked thoughtfully at one another.

Lily stood up, wiping her hands on her apron.

"Shall we walk around the garden?"

Jayne slipped her arm through Lily's as they strolled around the back garden, looking at the fruit trees coming into bud.

Then they wandered round to the front of the house to admire the daffodils.

They looked more glorious than ever, their golden trumpet heads filling the air with their scent.

"Let me cut you a bunch to take home," Lily said. Her faded blue eyes were bright as she handed her a large bouquet of daffodils. "Bonnie loved daffodils. She used to call them —"

"Daffies."

"Yes, that's right." She smiled as Jayne took the flowers from her. "Be careful going home; you have to get yourself back up that hill."

"I'll be fine, Lily, don't worry."

Lily reached out and touched her arm.

"You'll come again, won't you?"

"Yes, Lily. I'll definitely come again."

Jayne stood still for a moment, then suddenly stepped forward and gave Lily a hug. It felt warm and familiar, and for one crazy moment she didn't want to pull away.

"I'll look out for you," Lily said. "You're welcome any time. Look after that little baby, now."

* * * *

Jayne began her slow trek home up the hill, across the fields and down the footpath, away from the yellow house and back to the cottage she shared with Adam.

There was a feeling of contentment swelling inside her. She'd been inside the yellow house, seen Lily and talked with her. She didn't understand why she felt the way she did — at peace, somehow comforted.

She knew what Adam would say.

"You're pregnant. What do you expect?"

Could that really be the reason for feeling so complete, so totally in the right place at last?

* * * *

Lily wandered slowly back into her kitchen. A feeling of serenity and perfect calm crept over her for the first time in 40 years.

Gazing at the photograph of Bonnie sitting on her shelf, she gently traced the little girl's face with her fingers, and she smiled. ■

Kinsale, County Cork

Situated at the mouth of the River Bandon on the south-west coast lies Kinsale, one of 27 designated "Heritage Towns" in Ireland. Deriving its name from the Irish for "head of the sea" (Cionn tSáile), it has been a fishing port since mediaeval times. Fishing remains important, as does food. The town is known as the gourmet capital of Ireland and hosts an annual gourmet festival. Chef Keith Floyd was once a prominent local resident.

Tourists flock to the town not only to enjoy its scenery, historic buildings and independent shops, but also because it's an endpoint of the spectacular Wild Atlantic Way, the 2,500-km route around the Irish coastline, between Kinsale and Inishowen in Donegal.

Kinsale became a garrison town in the 1600s, and two forts can be seen along the bay. Today, it has a vision for the future. As the founding "Transition Town" in 2005, it was first to address the issue of how to build sustainable communities that don't depend on fossil fuels.

The Cup That Cheers

by Eirin Thompson

AT least take the child to visit the grave, Robbie," I overheard Auntie Penny say.

"Absolutely not," Dad replied, sounding cross.

"You're making it into a big deal by the very act of avoiding it, you know," she went on.

"I'd say it's a pretty big deal, being ten years old and the only kid in school without a mother on Mother's Day, wouldn't you?"

I ran out into the garden, then, and swung off the rope Uncle Joshua had tied to the big tree for me. I didn't want to hear any more.

My mum died when I was three. I barely remember her. I recall a yellow dress and a cloud of black hair and her holding a camera, but that's all.

Mum was the one who took all the pictures, so there aren't many of her, either. The only images I have of Mum are from the front, smiling. I don't know what she looked like from the side, or when she was sad.

They'd have done things differently if they'd known what was going to happen. If she'd been ill, they'd have had time to take more photographs.

But when you get knocked down crossing the road, you don't expect it – otherwise you just wouldn't cross that road that day.

"Mattie! Time for school!"

That's Dad. I could easily ride my bike to school by myself – it only takes five minutes. But he insists on coming, too. He worries about a car not seeing me, for obvious reasons.

Today is the Friday before Mother's Day, which means we'll be making cards in Art – it happens every year. I won't create a fuss.

*　*　*　*

Miss Donald is our substitute teacher, as Mrs Forbes is off on maternity leave, which means she's having a baby, if you didn't know. In

fact, she's already had the baby.

His name is Nicholas and she brought him into our class in his pram, but he just slept. I thought this meant she'd be coming back, but no – apparently she'd prefer to look after one baby than 29 ten-year-olds, which I can understand.

Anyway, I like Miss Donald. She has red hair – I mean scarlet, not ginger – and she ties it up in a big scarf round her head. Every afternoon, when we're tired, she tells us to put down our pencils while she reads to us.

We've had "Oliver Twist" and "The Wind In The Willows", and next she's going to read "Matilda", which was my mum's favourite when she was a child, Dad says, and is the reason I got my name.

The Matilda in the book is a child-genius, which I'm not, and a bookworm, which I am.

"OK, guys" – Miss Donald calls us "guys" – "time for Art. Pass your books up to the front and clear any clutter off your desks."

There's the usual racket while we do this, then we settle down.

"Now, who knows what day it is on Sunday? Hands up. Yes, Charlie?"

"Sunday."

A titter goes round the class. This is why Mrs Forbes never asked Charlie for his contribution, no matter how easy the question, but Miss Donald never seems to run out of patience with him.

"Sunday – yes, that's definitely the case. But what's special about this coming Sunday in particular? Charlotte?"

"It's Mothering Sunday."

"Well done – Mothering Sunday, or Mother's Day. And I have a super design for a card, which I hope you'll take pride in making and presenting to your mums.

"First, you're going to stick this print-out of a teapot to some gold card, cut around it, leaving a good hinge, and decorate it like a tea-cosy, using scraps of fabric and crepe paper.

"Inside, you're all going to attach a teabag and write the message, *This Mother's Day, have a cup of tea on me.*"

We got to work.

The school scissors aren't great – the hole is a bit too big to put just one finger through, yet too much of a squeeze for two – but I do the best I can. I am just doing a little bit of tidying up when Mrs Burt, the head teacher, comes in.

The room goes quiet – this always happens when Mrs Burt makes an appearance. It's like she casts a spell.

She is showing Miss Donald something in a folder, when she glances up and peeks at the front row to see what we are doing.

"Ah – Mother's Day cards," she observes, smiling at Charlotte. Then she casts her eye on the wider classroom.

She turns to Miss Donald and I hear her hiss: "Why is Matilda Smith making a card, Rachel? Don't you know about her situation?"

"What situation?" Miss Donald looks startled.

Mrs Burt turns to face the whiteboard, but I know what she is saying: Matilda Smith doesn't have a mother.

Miss Donald normally has a sweet face, but just now it looks like thunder. She is trying to keep her voice low, but I'm listening hard.

"I specifically came to you last week to check whether there could be anything problematic about making this an inclusive activity.

"I couldn't have asked you any more clearly. You assured me there were no issues."

I cannot hear what Mrs Burt says, but Miss Donald can barely conceal her rage. Then Mrs Burt looks at her folder, looks down the room, but not at me, and leaves.

Miss Donald takes a moment to compose herself, then wanders through the desks until she stops at mine.

"Nice trimming, Matilda."

She crouches down.

"I've just learned that this could be a bit of a tricky activity for you. I'm sorry. If I'd known, I'd have handled it more tactfully."

"It's all right," I say. "I don't mind. I like making things, anyway."

"Do you have anyone else you might like to celebrate with your card? Does your gran help to look after you, or your auntie?"

"Auntie Penny helps out, but it's really mostly down to Dad. He does all the stuff I suppose a mum would do – he makes dinner and washes the pots and cleans the bathroom and takes me to the library."

"Well, would you like to make your card for your dad, then?"

"Is that OK?"

"I really don't see why not. Does he drink tea?"

"Loads."

"A man after my own heart. Go for it!"

And so, on Mother's Day, I make Dad toast with butter and marmalade, put it on a tray with my card, and carry it upstairs to his bedroom.

"Mattie. What's all this?" he mumbles sleepily as he reaches for his watch.

"I've made you breakfast in bed," I explain. "And I have a card for you."

Dad looks confused. He scratches his head.

"Here – give me the tray and you open the curtains, so I can get a look at this." Dad props himself up on some pillows. "Shall I open this?"

"Yes! It's for you."

Dad takes out the teapot card and studies it. He opens it up and reads the verse. He smiles.

"Come here." He pulls me into a snuggly hug and kisses the top of my head.

"Whose idea was this?"

"Fifty per cent Miss Donald, fifty per cent me."

"Well, I one hundred per cent love it."

Now I smile.

"If you give me the teabag, I'll make you a cup to go with your toast."

"Oh, no, you don't. This is a very special teabag, and I'm keeping it for an occasion. Just use one of the regular ones for now."

✳   ✳   ✳   ✳

Later that day, Dad suggests we go for a drive.

"Where?" I ask.

"Well, I've been thinking," Dad explains. "And I'm wondering if Auntie Penny is right, and if I should take you to visit Mum's grave sometimes. Is that something you think you might want to do?"

My throat suddenly feels all dry, and it's hard to swallow.

"I thought you didn't like the graveyard."

"It's not that I don't like it. More that everyone there is . . . well . . . dead. I'm not sure what the point is, going there."

"I could go on my own, on my bike."

"No, Mattie, you couldn't. But if you want to go, I'll take you. When you were younger I thought it might upset you – that was all."

So Dad and I visit Mum's grave. Dad bought yellow roses at the garage shop, and I read the headstone, which said: *In loving memory of Joanna Smith, beloved wife of Robert, devoted mother of Matilda, died January 4, 2013.*

"It doesn't say rest in peace," I point out.

"No, it doesn't," Dad replies. "At the time, I think I still wanted her to fight back, cheat death and come home to us."

"But now you know that's not happening."

"Yep. Do you think I should ask the stonemason to add 'Rest In Peace'?"

"It might be nice."

The wind blows some flower-wrapping paper down from a group of people in the next aisle. Dad traps it with his foot.

"Sorry!"

I look up because it's a voice I think I know.

"Matilda! Hello, there!"

It's Miss Donald.

"She's my substitute teacher," I tell Dad.

"I think we're here on a similar mission," she says, coming over. "We lost our mum just before Christmas, so it's a tough day all round."

"I'm sorry to hear that," Dad says.

"She wasn't old – just sixty-three – but nowhere near as young as your wife."

"Mum was twenty-seven," I tell her.

"That's very sad," Miss Donald says.

"I liked my card," Dad tells her. "I believe it had something to do with you."

"If that has worked out at all well, then I'm grateful – I feared Matilda had been placed in a bad situation, through no fault of her own."

"You're a tough little bird, aren't you, Mattie?" Dad says.

"She's had to be," he adds, looking back at Miss Donald. "I'm Rob."

"It's nice to meet you, Rob. I'm Rachel." She puts out her hand.

Dad and Miss Donald stand and chat for a while, until she says, "I'd better go. I'm meant to be feeding my lot and I shouldn't keep them waiting."

"It was nice meeting you, Rachel," Dad replies. "I don't suppose you'd like to go out for a coffee some time?"

"Sold, if you make it a tea!" She smiles.

*   *   *   *

Auntie Penny is constantly asking me about Miss Donald. What age is she? What sort of hair does she have? Does she have kids?

"It's only you I'm concerned about in all this," she insists, although what harm Miss Donald's hair could do me I'm not at all sure.

Sometimes I tell Dad I'd like him to leave me with Penny and Joshua for a while, so I can swing on my rope. But that's not the only reason – I'm trying to leave the coast clear for him to see Miss Donald.

They've been out together a few times now, and it seems to be making Dad happy.

In a way, I'm lucky that all the pictures I have of Mum are of her smiling – I cannot even imagine her sad.

Miss Donald's different, though. She gets mad when people behave badly, or the kids are mean to each other, especially to Charlie, and that's OK, too – a living person can't always be content.

As I swing on my rope, I know that Miss Donald will never be my actual mum, but she could be my friend.

One of these days, I think Dad and Miss Donald might tell me they're an item, and that just might be the time for me to bring out the golden teapot card, and the real teapot, for the special occasion teabag. ■

Shutterstock.

Kilkenny Castle, Ireland

This castle has an incredible history going back to when it was first founded soon after the Norman conquests. Over the years it has been rebuilt, adapted and extended. Surrounded by 50 acres of rolling landscape, ornamental gardens, mature woodland and a man-made lake, it is home to an assortment of wildlife.

The 13th-century castle overlooking the River Nore came under the ownership of the Butler family when James, 3rd Earl of Ormond, bought the castle in 1391, and it remained with the family until it was sold to the State by Arthur, 6th Marquess and 24th Earl of Ormond, for just £50 in 1967. It is now owned by the people of Ireland.

King James II was just one notable guest who spent time here, in a sometimes dark history that includes the unsubstantiated tale that Alice Kyteler was imprisoned here before she was convicted of witchcraft. While she managed to flee to England, her associate, Petronilla de Meath, wasn't so lucky. Little wonder, then, that Kilkenny has been named one of Europe's most haunted places.

Crisis On The No. 7

by Barbara Dynes

ANNA sat on the bus, clutching her bag tightly. It was silly to be so tense, but she couldn't help it.

She glanced around her. There were only a handful of passengers, and her eyes were drawn to a tall, vaguely familiar woman, sitting at the front.

This number seven bus into town, though only every hour, was a boon for people living in her village, or "out in the wilds", as Jack, her grandson, put it.

Anna fidgeted, wishing she was on her usual weekly jaunt to get Bertie's special cat food, followed by a blow-dry, then a cuppa in Dolly's café. But today was going to be decidedly different.

Uneasily, she stared through the smeary window at the green patchwork of fields and trees, so familiar in the weak spring sunshine.

To be honest, she'd had serious second thoughts about this particular "mission".

She had been really keen – even excited – about it at first, so why was she now so sure it was a mistake?

Anna gazed at her fellow passenger. Neat grey hair, smart red scarf . . .

Ah, now she remembered! Kay, her name was: they'd been members of the same book club for a while. Kay, like herself, was retired and had obviously also given up driving.

Anna had gone over all the pros and cons carefully before making that decision, and didn't regret selling her car, with the traffic in town being such a nightmare, to say nothing of the parking.

After Don died, her daughter, Emily, had suggested that she moved "a bit nearer civilisation", but Anna decided against that.

OK, living in the wilds could be a teeny bit lonely at times, but Emily came when she could, and Jack, bless him, was for ever tearing up on his bike for flying visits.

Then there was Bertie, her gorgeous black cat. If she moved, how he'd miss his beloved woods and hate all the noise and bustle!

No, she was quite happy living alone; she'd always prided herself on being the self-sufficient, confident type. But being so nervous about today hardly spelled confidence, did it?

She forced herself to think about something else. What if they took this bus off, due to lack of customers? Everyone would be really stuck!

She would probably cope, though; she was quite proficient on her laptop and ordering her groceries online worked very well.

And Emily was always willing to ferry her to appointments.

Anna was suddenly jolted forward in her seat – this bus seemed to be juddering a lot more than usual today. Or maybe it was just her nerves causing the juddering. She grinned and gave herself a little shake.

When you're tense, Anna, you do tend to exaggerate everything, she told herself.

She must stop overreacting and calm down.

But, the next minute, a terrible grating noise set her teeth on edge. The bus skewed alarmingly, then came to a shuddering stop. There followed a scary silence.

Her heart hammering, Anna grovelled on the floor for her handbag.

Ted, the driver, appeared at the front of the bus, an anxious expression on his usually cheery face.

"Is everyone all right?"

Anna, along with her fellow passengers, reassured him.

"We've broken down; I'll have to call the depot," Ted declared. "They'll send another bus out in two ticks. We won't be stuck here for long, ladies!"

Ups And Downs

Up! I see the neighbour's cat
Thinking, "What on earth is that?"
Down! The lawn is full of moss –
That'll make the gardener cross.

Up! I'll give next door a shout,
Busy hanging washing out.
Down! I've disappeared from view.
Just had time for, "How'd you do?"

Up! And in the guttering
Lies the ball we lost last spring.
Down! Poor dolly's on the path:
Looks as if she needs a bath.

Oops! The children home from school.
Hope that I don't look a fool.
"Grandma, you're a jumping bean.
You can share our trampoline!"

Tessa-Jo Stone

"Two ticks" might have been a bit optimistic, Anna surmised, seeing as they were only just past Willow Bend. But it couldn't be helped, of course.

Ted went back to the driver's seat to the phone and Anna watched as Kay rummaged in her bag and brought out her mobile.

Anna sat back, thinking hard. She had allowed plenty of time so she wouldn't be late, but . . .

Fate, you could call it – this breakdown. It was amazing how, sometimes in life, things took an unexpected turn.

This hitch seemed like an omen, giving her a way out and showing that she could now, reasonably and honourably, cancel everything.

She had a contact number for Mrs Jenkins – she would phone and explain, apologise profusely, adding that she'd decided such a project wasn't for her after all.

Then she would get off this bus, cross the road and wait for the

number seven going back. She closed her eyes and tried to relax, expecting the tension to drain away.

But it didn't, not completely. Why was that? Guilt, of course; she'd be letting people down and she felt really bad about that. Well, it couldn't be helped.

Anna took out her phone. But Kay was moving down the bus towards her, dropping her own mobile back into her bag as she did so.

Sliding into the seat next to Anna, she leaned across, a worried expression on her pale face.

"How long d'you think we'll be? Only I need to be in town by two o'clock."

"Oh, I'm sure Ted will soon sort it." Anna smiled. "I've decided to go home, anyway."

But Kay was not listening.

"Look, I'm so sorry, but could I possibly borrow your phone, please?"

she asked anxiously.

"Mine's not charged up – I never do remember to do it! They'll think I'm not coming.

"At work, I mean; I do voluntary work for the homeless shelter," she explained. "I'm Kay. I think I remember your face from the book club, don't I?"

"Yes. I'm Anna."

Anna handed over her mobile. She was in no rush to make her own call; she could ring once she was on the return bus. She felt awful about having to phone with her excuses.

She might be old-fashioned, but phoning – in circumstances like this – always seemed a bit cowardly. It was much better to talk to people face to face. But what else could she do?

"You could wait for the new bus, face Mrs Jenkins and tell her exactly why you've made such a negative decision," a little voice in her head said.

But Anna ignored it.

Kay tapped at the numbers.

"Thanks so much," she said a few minutes later, handing back the phone. "I've only just taken on this job, cooking meals and helping out.

"But I was really doubtful about it at first and thought I'd never cope! The other volunteers knew how I felt, you see, and I don't want them to think I've walked away!

"I really enjoy it now – I've made so many friends. Your own trip to town wasn't urgent, I hope?"

Anna shook her head. Kay obviously wanted to talk and it seemed unkind to leave her here, waiting alone.

OK, she'd miss the next bus back, but so what? There was only the faithful Bertie waiting for her.

"Believe it or not, I was going into town to join a choir," Anna blurted out.

"Pardon?"

Anna watched Kay's eyebrows rise and realised how absurd that statement sounded.

"Crazy, eh?" Anna went on. "Not exactly a worthwhile mission, like your job. It's just . . . I saw an advert online for singers.

"It's just an amateur group, but they go around entertaining in old people's homes and day centres, that sort of thing. I used to love singing, years ago –"

Kay looked encouraging.

"That's great! So what's gone wrong?"

Anna shrugged and looked away.

"I suppose you could say I've lost my nerve."

"Another bus on the way, ladies!" Ted shouted. "Won't be long now!"

"Great, thanks!" Kay called back, then looked critically at Anna.

"Really? I don't mean to be rude, but I don't remember you as the nervous type."

Anna shrugged. No, she was usually quite the opposite . . . till that phone call. She shuddered.

A member of the choir had rung: a very friendly-sounding lady called Julie.

"I just thought I'd give you a call to welcome you to the fold," she began cheerily.

Julie had gone on to explain that members went out for meals and social outings in between the entertaining.

It all sounded wonderful – new friends were exactly what Anna hoped for.

But then, just before saying goodbye, Julie casually dropped her bombshell.

Anna turned to Kay.

"You're quite right; I'm not normally this panicky," she said. "But one of the choir members rang and, guess what?

"She casually let on that she was once a soprano with the BBC choir! A professional singer, if you please. The BBC choir, Kay!

"What on earth will they make of my attempts, if that's the standard they're used to?

"I've only ever been rank amateur –"

"So what? They won't all be stars, Anna," Kay declared. "My old mum used to say that we should always make the most of any small talent we have.

"That's what I reminded myself when I nearly gave up on this job.

"My small talent happens to be cooking; I make a really mean spaghetti bolognese." Kay giggled.

Then she looked at Anna.

"And, thinking of Mum," she continued, "when she finally went into a home, she couldn't remember much at all, yet she was word-perfect with all the old songs.

"The staff led a regular sing-along, and those sessions really kept Mum going," Kay added pointedly. "They were the highlight of her week, something she really looked forward to."

Anna smiled. Kay was obviously trying to tell her something.

Suddenly, out of the blue, she recalled a family wedding she had attended a while back.

After one hymn, Jack had turned to her and whispered, "Gran, I had no idea you could sing like that. Awesome!"

A little flutter of delight went through her even now – her grandson rarely praised anyone!

Ted appeared again.

"The replacement bus is here!"

"Thanks so much," Kay said. "Coming, Anna?"

Anna took a deep breath. What had been her own mother's favourite saying?

"Seize any opportunity, Anna."

She followed Kay off the bus and stepped eagerly on to the new one. That original excitement was back.

Of course she could do it! ■

A Pair Of White Gloves

by Teresa Ashby

YOU look stunning," Dad says and I smile nervously. "I can't believe an ugly old thing like me has such a beautiful daughter, but we have your mum to thank for that. You look so like her, Ruth." His eyes shimmer as they always do when he talks about my mum.

"I wish she was here, Dad," I say and my throat tightens as I struggle not to cry. It took my best friend, Angel, ages to do my hair and make-up. She'll kill me if I undo all her good work.

"Well, as you know I've never been much of a believer, but I do believe she is watching over you today and every day."

I nod and take some deep breaths. I wish I could believe that, too.

"How about me?" he asks. "Have I scrubbed up OK? Do I look fit to walk you up the aisle?"

I laugh.

"You look very handsome, Dad. Not an ugly old thing at all. Have you got your speech?"

He taps his chest.

"It's in here," he says. "My words will come from my heart."

"You are soppy," I say.

"The car will be here for the bridesmaids soon," he says. "I'd better check they're all ready to go. Do you need anything?"

"I have everything I need, Dad."

My bedroom doesn't look much like my bedroom any more. I've

Illustration by Jim Dewar.

already moved a lot of my stuff to our new flat, but there are a few things left here. Things I haven't got round to sorting out yet.

I stand at the window looking out on the street where I grew up. I used to draw hopscotch grids on the pavement with Mum's dressmaker's chalk.

"You little pickle," she'd say and then she'd come out and have a game with me.

"Oh, Mum, I wish you were here."

I wish I could believe, like Dad, that she was still around somewhere.

I open the window and breathe in the fresh spring air. The sun is shining for us and I'm hoping we don't get any April showers.

There's a light breeze, but it strengthens suddenly and blows the curtains into the room, knocking a table lamp over. The lamp hits a pile of boxes and the shoe box on the top falls to the floor.

The curtains settle again and I close the window quickly and turn to see my collection of white gloves amid scraps of yellowing tissue paper scattered about the floor.

* * * *

When I was a child, the best thing about Easter for me wasn't the chocolate eggs, but the pair of white gloves my mum always bought me for church.

They weren't plain white gloves either, but always a bit fancy. I loved the feel of them, as they were always snug around my fingers, unlike the woolly mittens I wore all through the winter.

I suppose the gloves were a symbol of warmer weather and lighter

61

clothes. Every year I'd get a new pair, and when summer came, the gloves would go into a shoe box with all the rest.

I wrapped each pair carefully in white tissue paper.

"You're a funny little stick," my mum said when she saw my collection. "Fancy keeping those old gloves."

But they weren't just any old gloves. The smallest pair reminded me of when my baby brother, Craig, came to church with us for the first time. He bawled all through the service.

The next pair had a thin navy blue stripe at the edge of each finger. They were a very snug fit. I loved them. The new young vicar loved them, too.

I thought he was wonderful, Reverend Petrie. He had long hair and was so different from our old vicar who had barely any hair at all.

He had a screen at the front of the church and he said, "Why are you all sitting so far from each other? Come forward, brothers and sisters. You won't be able to see the words all the way back there."

The screen was like the one we had at school for assemblies.

Mum seemed quite excited as she ushered me forward, but some of the older ladies muttered and grumbled as they moved seats.

That day we sang "Michael, Row The Boat Ashore". It was fabulous. At last here was a hymn I could enjoy singing, and sing I did at the top of my voice.

"What's wrong with 'All Things Bright And Beautiful', that's what I want to know," Mrs Evans said, but I thought I'd never seen her cheeks as rosy.

When we'd finished singing, he told us the origins of the song, how it had connections with the slave trade and the civil rights movement.

I was full of questions as we walked home. What was the slave trade and what were civil rights?

Mum said good people had fought for what was right all through time and they would never stop. She always loved me asking questions and sometimes her answers were rather long-winded, but she was passionate about history and, because of her, I became passionate about it, too.

As I got older, white gloves became harder to come by and I didn't go to church so often. Sometimes I'd go along to keep Mum company and I didn't mind because Reverend Petrie's sermons were always interesting.

Then, when I was seventeen, Reverend Petrie introduced us to his nephew, Dominic. He looked fed up and embarrassed, as if he'd rather be anywhere in the world than there.

"Dominic is staying with me for a while," he said. "I'm sure everyone will make him welcome." He looked at me when he said that and raised one of his eyebrows.

"Ruth would love to show him round," Mum said.

"History is an interest of Dominic's," Reverend Petrie went on. "Perhaps you'd like to show him our village agricultural museum, Ruth. I believe they're open this afternoon for a couple of hours."

Dominic was very good looking and had the same gentle deep brown eyes as his uncle, but his mouth was turned down at the corners and I wasn't about to be fixed up by my mum and the vicar.

"I'll have to check if I'm free," I said airily.

"Ruth will call for you at three," Mum said and Dominic muttered grudging thanks.

I told Mum off as we walked home. How dare she try to set me up with the vicar's nephew, who clearly didn't want to be set up.

"What on earth makes you think I'd do a thing like that?" she said.

"I'm not supposed to tell you, but Dominic's parents were killed in an accident and Reverend Petrie is the closest family he has."

I was shocked.

"Why didn't you tell me before?"

"Because Dominic doesn't want everyone to know. He's worried people will pity him.

"Remember when Reverend Petrie went away suddenly? He was sorting out the funeral and other things and he brought Dominic home with him."

"He looks old enough to take care of himself," I said.

"I can't believe you said that, Ruth. He lost his parents. How do you think that feels?"

I felt awful for being so unfeeling. But I couldn't suddenly start being nice to him or he'd know I knew, so I went to call for him at three.

"We don't have to go anywhere," he said as we left the vicarage. "If you've got stuff to do, don't let me keep you."

"I was planning a museum trip soon anyway," I said. "I'm doing a project about agricultural labourers since we seem to have a lot in our family tree."

"For school?"

"No, for me. I like history. You can blame my mum and your uncle for that. Every sermon he does has a history lesson. I always come away feeling as if I've learned something."

"I suppose that's what religion is, isn't it?" he said. "History. I'm doing economics at university. I suppose you think that sounds boring."

"Whatever floats your boat," I said. "If you'd rather have a coffee or something, there's a good café in the village."

"Perhaps we could do both," he said. "I'll buy you a coffee as a thank you for showing me the museum."

"Even if you're not interested." I laughed.

"I didn't say that I wasn't," he said. "I do find history interesting."

I forgot to be annoyed about being forced to spend the afternoon with Dominic and I forgot about feeling sorry for him. As it turned out, we got along really well. At the end of the day he thanked me.

"You know about my parents?" he asked as he walked me home.

"I'm sorry," I said. "I can't imagine how that must feel."

"I don't want to talk about it," he said.

I wouldn't say I fell in love with him that afternoon. That came the following year when he came home from university for the summer. Mum was as pleased as Punch, and I think Reverend Petrie was, too, when we started dating.

A year later Mum died suddenly. She hadn't even been ill. She was there and then she wasn't and I was numb with shock. Dominic rushed home to be with me. He seemed to know all the right things to say to Dad and my brother and he encouraged me to cry.

"I'm afraid if I start to cry, I'll never stop," I said.

"I know," he said. "But it's not good to bottle it up inside, Ruth. It will eat away at you. Believe me; I know how bad that is."

My eyes felt at times as if they were burning with unshed tears, but I couldn't let them go.

Reverend Petrie gave a wonderful funeral service. He made us laugh as he recalled the day Mum corrected him when he'd got a historical point slightly wrong in his sermon.

It was afterwards, when everyone had gone home and I stood out in the garden, that it hit me that I would never see Mum again and I crumpled, but Dominic was there, catching me before I fell, cradling me in his arms and telling me to let it out.

* * * *

Four years have passed since then and not a day goes by that I don't think about Mum. Today I have been thinking of her since the moment I woke up, imagining how excited she would be and how pleased that I was marrying the nephew of her favourite vicar.

Every time I pull on my white gloves at work, I think of her. She'd be overjoyed to see me working in a big museum, having to wear gloves to handle delicate old things.

I sigh and bend down to gather up the gloves, carefully folding them in their tissue paper, but I find a pair I don't remember seeing before. They are white, elbow length and made with satin and lace, and the tissue paper around them is pristine white. A note falls from the paper.

My darling Ruth. You don't look at your white gloves these days, but I saw these and had to get them for you. If you ever get married, I can imagine you'll look for the perfect pair and I will tell you to look in your shoe box. You can come and give me a hug now. Mum xxx.

If only I could give her a hug!

I didn't even look at gloves because Mum had always bought them for me for special occasions, and it would have felt wrong to buy my own.

But these are from her and they feel so right. I pull them on and the soft, silky fabric hugs my hands.

Angel appears in the doorway and lets out a wail.

"Don't cry! You'll ruin your make-up!"

"Too late." I'm laughing, too. I'm laughing because I know Mum is watching over me, and while Angel dabs and blots and reapplies my mascara, I explain about the gloves.

As I walk across the little green to the church with Dad I can feel Mum's presence all around us for the first time since she passed away.

She's always with us, just like Dad said, and I will hold her in my heart for ever. ∎

Liathach from Loch Clair, Highland

The peaceful summer view of Liathach from Loch Clair gives little indication of the challenges that await the serious Munro-bagger keen to add Liathach's two peaks, Spidean a'Choire Lèith and Mullach an Rathain, to their collection.

The mountain is known to some as "the beast of Torridon", while the ridge of rocky pinnacles that joins the two peaks rejoices in the forbidding name of Am Fasarinen (the Teeth)! There are said to be almost no descents from those teeth, so once underway, intrepid hikers just have to keep going along the ridge to the other end.

Advice from other hikers talks about a "relentless ascent" with gradients varying from "very steep to very, very steep".

You don't have to be a skilled mountaineer to make the most of the area, though. Those not so energetically inclined will be glad to enjoy the mountain scenery from ground level on the lovely five-and-a-half-mile circular walk around the shores of Loch Clair and neighbouring Loch Coulin!

Happy Ever After

by Patsy Collins

T HAT'S Mike over there," Dorinda said. "What do you think?"
Looking in the direction her friend was pointing, Carrie spotted a
pleasant-looking man with freckles and dark hair, who barely
matched her own five feet five inches.

"Um, he's, um . . ." Her hesitation wasn't so much to do with
Mike's rather ordinary appearance as the fact she recognised him.

Hard not to when he'd been at every party or social event Carrie had
attended in recent weeks. Whenever she'd caught sight of him he'd been
surrounded by a group of laughing friends.

Mike being sociable and popular wasn't a problem, exactly. Not unless
Carrie's suspicions were correct and Dorinda was trying to get the two of
them together.

"I want you to be as happy as me, Carrie," she'd said. "To have
someone who makes me feel the way I do with Bill."

That was fine in theory. Bill was outgoing, generous and entertaining.
He was spontaneous, lively and fun. Absolutely perfect for Dorinda.

Trouble was, Dorinda didn't seem to realise the kind of man who made
her own pulse race with excitement would have Carrie's pounding in
nervous alarm. Mike was Bill's brother and Dorinda had assured her
that although he lacked a few of his brother's inches, his personality
didn't come up short.

It was the combination of these good points and the way Dorinda
mentioned them so frequently, along with the fact that Mike was
inexplicably single, which had Carrie worried. That and Dorinda being
practically impossible to say no to.

They'd met at junior school. Dorinda had raced out on to the
playground making a commotion.

"Come and play, everyone!" she'd yelled.

Carrie, following after her, had picked up Dorinda's dropped hair
ribbon and returned it.

Illustration by Ruth Blair.

"Thanks. We're best friends now." She'd immediately begun to swing her skipping rope around the two of them and they'd jumped in unison.

It had been like that ever since. Dorinda was the one who had ideas, started things, took centre stage. Carrie formed the supporting cast. She'd been happy joining in childhood games and perfectly content to tag along to pubs, clubs and parties as they grew up.

Carrie enjoyed listening to the chatter and music, but couldn't start a conversation herself or get up and dance until there were so many others on the floor that she felt more conspicuous sitting down.

Since their teens, Dorinda had always had a boyfriend, but she had time for Carrie, too. They even double dated a few times. The boys Dorinda attracted were very like her and as a result no-one noticed that Carrie barely said a word.

Even when Dorinda's relationship with Bill became serious, it didn't alter the friendship between the two. They went out together, or stayed in chatting or watching a film, when Bill was at rugby practice or drinking with his team mates. Carrie joined her friend in cheering him on at matches and occasionally the three of them shared a meal.

Of course, Dorinda and Bill spent a lot of time on their own, and that was fine. Much as Carrie enjoyed being with Dorinda, she liked time away from her, too. A chance to sit still and be quiet. To shut out reality and lose herself in a book.

The same would be true of a man like Mike; she'd need more time away from him than was compatible with a long-term relationship.

Why put herself through all the pressure and angst if there was no chance of a happy ever after? Plus, as he was Bill's brother, it would be hard to avoid him after it all went wrong. That would be horribly awkward.

None of this seemed to have occurred to Dorinda and she jumped and waved until Mike detached himself from his friends and came over to be introduced.

He gave Carrie a lovely smile.

"Nice to meet you finally, after hearing so many good things about you," he said.

So it wasn't just Carrie who'd been on the receiving end of either Dorinda or Bill's hints that they should get together. Luckily Mike seemed no more convinced than she was that they were suited and after a few words of polite conversation, he slipped away.

That didn't deter the matchmakers. Over the next few weeks, Carrie often encountered Mike at her friend's home, or places they went together.

He was always pleasant to her, but generally kept a good distance between them and skilfully switched the conversation if either Dorinda or his brother seemed to be leading it into awkward territory.

Those meetings weren't too difficult. She found that Mike's remarks often provoked a burst of conversation from anyone else present and all she had to do was smile, nod and occasionally add a word of agreement to seem to be taking part.

That didn't help when she bumped into Mike in the bookshop. She'd come to like him and naturally didn't wish to appear rude so, gathering her courage, Carrie approached and asked how he was.

"Fine. You, too, I hope?"

"Yes."

"Good."

At that point the assistant finished serving another customer.

"Hi, Carrie. I've put by a couple of books I think you might be interested in." She gestured to a shelf behind the counter.

"No need to ask if you come here often, then," Mike said.

"No. I mean yes, I do."

"More of a Kindle man myself, but I wanted to get something for Mum's birthday. Haven't got a clue, though."

"You could give her a book token?"

"They still sell those?"

Carrie nodded.

"I will, then. Good idea. Thanks."

He'd bought his tokens and a card before Carrie finished looking through the books which had been set aside for her. Even so, he hadn't left the shop by the time she'd paid for the three she wanted.

"Do you have time for a coffee?" Mike asked.

Again Carrie nodded. And when the lad in the coffee shop said, "Your usual?" as they reached the counter, she even managed to smile.

"I come here quite often, too."

She accepted his offer of cake; it would give her something to hide

Counting My Blessings

There's cheery looks and travel books
And warm scents on the breeze;
There's sunny days and Shakespeare's plays
And countless types of cheese.
There's ice-cream cones and garden gnomes
And stories of romance;
There's gorgeous food (especially pud)
And partners at a dance.
Of course, we do have down days, too
And sometimes we feel sad,
But I would say life, in its way,
Is really not too bad.

Ewan Smith

behind and an excuse not to say much.

They smiled at each other, sipped their drinks and ate their cakes for a few minutes. A couple of times she thought he was about to speak.

"Carrie, this is a bit awkward," he said finally, "but . . . well, I think Bill and Dorinda are trying to fix us up."

"I think so, too."

"You seem nice, but I can see we're very different and it wouldn't work out."

"That's what I thought," she mumbled into her cherry sponge.

When she glanced up, he looked relieved.

"So we're allies?"

Carrie nodded yet again, and as he offered his hand, she shook it.

"We should tell them, I suppose," he said.

"I have tried, but it's hard to dissuade Dorinda once she gets an idea into her head."

"Bill's as bad."

"I think they only talk each other out of things by coming up with an even wackier scheme. Maybe that's what we need?" Carrie suggested.

With the pressure off and a common purpose, talking to Mike wasn't really so difficult.

"OK. So, how about next time they try, we pretend to go along with it and fall for each other? We'd have to go out a few times to make it look convincing, but maybe's there's a film or something we'd both like to see. Then we break up in some spectacular fashion and are so broken-hearted they never try again?"

"I wouldn't want to make them feel bad." Neither could she imagine herself doing anything in a "spectacular fashion".

"No, of course not. So not broken-hearted; we'll just let them see that we're not really suited?"

"OK. Yes." And hopefully Dorinda would also realise that her other friends were equally unsuitable as boyfriends for Carrie and this situation wouldn't arise again.

✳ ✳ ✳ ✳

The first part of their plan went extremely well and was actually rather fun. She and Mike, when they were next pushed together, found a quiet corner and gazed into each other's eyes.

They grinned conspiratorially, checked for when they were being watched and put on a bit of a performance. Even to her, it seemed almost real. Except Carrie wouldn't have been able to think of anything much to say, nor been brave enough to occasionally touch his arm in a flirtatious manner, if he'd really been chatting her up.

As Mike suggested, they saw a film together. Neither said much as they watched, as they had both read the book and were eager to see how it matched up.

"I recognised the character names, but that was about it!" Mike said afterwards.

"Be fair, they only changed three parts of the story," Carrie replied.

"You think?"

"Yep. Beginning, middle and end!"

His snort of laughter was very unlike his usual controlled chuckles.

"Why don't people just write new stories, if they don't like the originals?" Carrie asked.

"Beats me. Mind you, it's even worse when they change history or the characters of real people."

"That makes me so mad!"

They'd walked to the pub, had three drinks each, eaten two rounds of sandwiches and shared the last slice of Black Forest gateau, before they'd named all the most terrible examples they could think of and devised suitable punishments for the scriptwriters responsible.

Mike walked her home.

"How about we go for a proper meal on Saturday, instead of risking whatever the Red Lion has left?"

Carrie temporarily forgot why he was asking and was delighted he wanted to see her again.

"I'd like that, but I promised Dorinda I'd go to the rugby club with her and Bill." Saying their names reminded her this date had just been for their benefit.

"Oh, yes. The reception their sponsors have organised. I'd forgotten about that. See you there, then."

"OK. Bye, then." She rushed in before her disappointment became obvious and embarrassed them both.

Carrie felt better the following day when Mike sent a text thanking her for her company and suggesting he pick her up on Saturday. OK, she realised why, but it would still be nice to chat to him on the drive there and home again.

*   *   *   *

Mike made sure to monopolise Carrie's attention during the rugby club event. It wasn't difficult for her to play her part; Mike was fun.

During the dull speeches he entertained her with daft jokes, generally at his own expense and all whispered in her ear. Even better, on the way home he suggested an alternative date for them to go out for dinner.

Carrie took care not to make him feel uncomfortable by seeming too eager.

"Actually I'm supposed to be seeing Dorinda then, too, but yes, let's go out then. Standing her up can be part of the payback for fixing us up."

"Right. Yes, teach her a lesson." He sounded hurt.

Oh, dear. In trying to hide how keen she was to see him again, she'd made it seem as though she'd really rather not.

"I'm sorry . . . I didn't . . ."

"Carrie, it's OK." He reached over and squeezed her hand. "I understand."

*   *   *   *

Neither of them had been to the Greek restaurant before, nor knew much about it, but they couldn't have chosen anywhere better to avoid the evening becoming awkward. Alexandros's Taverna had that night been open for exactly a year and the manager was marking the anniversary.

The place was packed and the atmosphere celebratory. The food was served in lots of tiny courses, very tasty and beautifully presented. That gave them a safe topic of conversation, though it was hardly needed.

Throughout the meal there was a great deal of bouzouki playing, folk singing and dancing, even some plate smashing. Although that last one seemed to have been an accident on the part of a rushing waiter, it was enthusiastically applauded.

On the way home, they discussed it.

"I've heard that plate-smashing used to be traditional at Greek dinners, but I didn't think I'd ever see it happen."

"Me neither. Everyone seemed to enjoy it, didn't they? I hope that means the waiter won't get into trouble."

"I shouldn't think he will. Carrie, talking of breaking things . . ."

Oh, no! She knew they'd be staging a break-up soon, but was hoping they'd go out at least once more first.

"Do you know why Bill and Dorinda were so keen to persuade you to go out with me?" Mike asked.

"They just wanted us to be as happy as them and couldn't see we're too different for that to work."

"Yeah . . . that's what I thought."

Why prolong the agony by going over it again?

"So how do we show them they were wrong?"

"We don't. I've already told them," Mike said.

"Oh." It was for the best, she supposed. Carrie was too shy and quiet for someone like Mike, except that she wasn't so much when she was with him.

And was he quite as outgoing as he seemed, or did he, like her, smile and nod on the edges of a group? She'd heard him start off conversations by soliciting opinions, but she couldn't recall him taking part in the resulting debates.

It was Carrie who'd approached him in the bookshop. At all those clubs and parties where she'd seen him laughing with friends, she'd been doing the same, hadn't she?

"What did they say?" Carrie asked.

"That I was talking rubbish. That they'd known us a very long time and know what we're really like. They have a point, don't they?" Mike took her hand. "I mean, you prefer paperbacks and I love my Kindle, but we both read the same books."

"And you favour green and I go for black, but we both like olives."

"Exactly."

"But I thought . . . What did you mean when you said, 'talking about breaking things'?"

"I was trying to confess that this conversation took place before our first date and . . . I was in on the fixing up. So I can't very well tell them it was a bad idea, can I? Not even if I wanted to."

"I suppose not. Guess we'll have to stay together for ever?" Carrie asked.

"Forced into it, I reckon," Mike said.

"Only in the film version."

"Ah, the book might end differently?" Mike asked. "True. 'They all lived happily ever after' is traditional."

"I do like a bit of tradition," Carrie remarked.

"Me, too."

"I believe kissing is also traditional at this point."

"I thought you were supposed to be the shy one?" Mike said. ■

Shutterstock.

Osborne, Isle Of Wight

Standing majestically in extensive grounds with walled gardens, complete with trained fruit trees, through to wildflower meadows and mature cedar trees, the former residence of Queen Victoria proved the ideal place for the Royal Family to enjoy perfect summer days.

It was a place where she, Prince Albert and their nine children were able to relax. Queen Victoria would take therapeutic dips in the Solent, thanks to a private beach and bathing wagon ensuring privacy, and she also enjoyed painting in the grounds while the children played in the Swiss Cottage and tended their own garden.

The estate was initially leased, then bought in May 1845 for £28,000 from Lady Isabella Blachford. However, the original house proved too small and the old house was demolished and a new one built – this was on the advice of Thomas Cubitt, and he proceeded to design the new house in collaboration with Prince Albert. This included the opulent Durbar Wing, built by John Lockwood Kipling (Rudyard Kipling's father) and Bhai Ram Singh.

The interior of Osborne is a warren of rooms, from the children's nursery with cots lined in a row, through to Queen Victoria's bed chamber, where she passed away in 1901. It's not difficult to see why Osborne held such a special place in her heart.

The Pilgrim's Tale

by H. Johnson-Mack

THE year was marching towards midsummer and one of the church's oldest celebratory feasts, that of St John the Baptist. Coinciding with summer solstice, it was a time of merrymaking, light and hope for the whole community, the last hurrah before the hard slog of harvest would begin.

So it was only fitting that the sun, woefully absent for too many days this month, should make a reappearance in time for it.

But no.

Sister Ursula, the staunch little infirmarian of Langlois convent, glanced heavenwards, showers falling from colourless clouds dousing her face. Clucking her tongue, she joined the rest of her sisters in chapel for Prime service.

The no-nonsense celleress, Sister Donata, grinned at her wrinkled nose.

"You look like you've swallowed a thistle."

"'Tis this rain, not prickles, that has me looking sour," Ursula muttered. "It plays havoc with my knees, not to mention my herbs."

"Then I will cease praying for rain for the crops, and ask for sunshine instead. We can't have you suffering, especially with new patients on your hands."

"New patients?"

Donata's brows rose.

"What, have they not called on you yet? A well-dressed pilgrim and his

Illustration by Jim Dewar.

mother have arrived, and he looks in need of your ministrations before they can continue their journey."

Her eyes twinkled as, raising a hand to shield her words, she added, "He's a handsome young gentleman, too, Sister. Some folk have all the luck . . ."

*　　*　　*　　*

Donata was right about one thing, Ursula reflected as she sought out her potential patient after the service. Despite unnatural pallor, the pilgrim was certainly personable.

As to luck, after spending just minutes with his mother, a shrewish woman with a voice as sharp as her nose, well, that was debatable.

"Your prioress tells us you have royal connections," she announced, examining Ursula's hands before allowing access to her son.

Ursula hid a smile at the elegant Prioress Osyth's description of Langlois's tenuous link with King Henry Plantagenet, thanks to Ursula's care of him when he was a fiery prince at war with the former king, Stephen.

"Rest assured, I have skills enough to care for your son." She turned a kinder countenance to her patient, whose skin showed unpleasant signs of fever.

"Now, young man."

"My name is Segar Velyn," he mumbled, struggling up on one elbow, "and this is my mother, Lady Edith."

Ursula inclined her head in acknowledgement before she set about examining the handsome youth. No visible injury, but signs of fever, a little malnourishment – surprising in one clearly well-bred – and something more.

"You seem wearied," she observed.

Segar's eyes were vacant.

"I do not sleep."

Frowning, Ursula continued her examination.

"That's a striking pendant," she remarked, indicating the curled snake hung round his neck, two topaz jewels for eyes.

He grasped it almost savagely.

"A Glain Nedre," he muttered. "My talisman."

His fingers trembled as he cradled the snake jewel, a Welsh piece considered to be a sacred charm.

"You are on pilgrimage?" Ursula asked as she readied a chamomile tincture, dusted with a little ash and aconite.

It was Lady Edith who replied.

"Yes, to Lindisfarne. My husband was about to go on pilgrimage before he died. As he now cannot make the journey, we go for him."

"A laudable mission." Ursula extended her hand to the young man. "Now, come rest in my infirmary, and you'll be back on the road again in no time."

✳   ✳   ✳   ✳

A while later, Ursula stood looking down at the sleeping Segar. It relieved her to see him free, for a while at least, of whatever was giving him that strained look.

Was that what made her doubt Lady Edith's story? Or was it the expression on Segar's face when his mother talked of their homage to his late father?

Well, whatever his troubles, he could enjoy a little respite here in Ursula's kingdom, if only from the strident Lady Edith. The woman had reluctantly agreed to leave him in the little nun's care, largely thanks to Bridget's stout support of her mentor.

The recollection made Ursula smile. There were not many who could stand against the earnest innocence of her apprentice, including, it seemed, Edith Velyn.

Well, she couldn't stand gazing at fallen angels all day. She had her rounds to make in Becenan, the valley demesne in which Langlois dwelt, and the constable's wife to check on after a slip had resulted in a nasty swollen ankle.

She had just finished restocking her medicine basket when she heard Bridget shriek.

Next moment, the novice shot into the stillroom, followed by an unknown male voice calling, "Mademoiselle?"

Touching a palm to Bridget's cheek, Ursula entered the infirmary, where a slim man, as dark as Velyn was fair, leaned over his sleeping form. He jumped when he saw the little nun.

"Forgive me, I didn't mean to startle anyone."

"My assistant is skittish," Ursula explained. "Like a fawn in a forest, frightened into flight by the arrival of man."

She felt her own hackles rise as a spark of interest lit the stranger's eyes.

"Can I help you?" she asked sharply. He reluctantly drew his gaze from the stillroom.

"I've cut my hand, and was told someone could care for it here."

After a pause, Ursula waved him to the larger hearth in the long room, where a fire burned low to keep out the damp.

"You are the second young man I've tended today," she remarked as she applied yarrow to a split palm. "Are you on pilgrimage, too?"

The man glanced at the sleeping Segar, then grimaced.

"Nothing so worthy. I'm an apprentice journeyman, on my way to find masonry jobs."

Ursula ran a thumb over his work-roughened skin.

"Learning a vital trade is admirable enough. There! All patched up."

The smile he gave her transformed his face.

"Thank you, Sister . . ."

"Ursula," she replied, shaking the hand still in hers. "Now, Master Journeyman, I must shoo you out of my sickroom."

He bowed.

"Of course. And it's Laisney, Sister. Ahren Laisney."

∗   ∗   ∗   ∗

Emerging from the woodland path into the full light of day, Ursula noted in amusement that Donata's prayers had been answered.

With the welcome appearance of the sun, it was now warm in the valley, so she wished for something lighter than her hood as she made her way downhill towards Becenan's moat-ringed manor at the heart of the wooded demesne.

Though not her favourite season, she could appreciate the glow summer brought to trees, fields and flowers and enjoy being amongst it all.

Becenan was bustling when she arrived. There were the usual servants going about their tasks of cooking, cleaning and caring for chickens trying to escape their handler on the drawbridge, all to the music of the blacksmith's hammer.

Several men were building a huge bonfire on the sward before the manor walls, led by Becenan's redoubtable constable, tall, flaxen-haired Magnuss the Dane. At the sight of Ursula, he jogged over, calling out a cheery greeting.

"You are here to see my Estrid?"

"That I am," Ursula confirmed. "How does she fare?"

"She is well, Sister," Magnuss replied, a softening expression revealing his affection for his wife. "And scolding me for fussing over her."

Ursula chuckled, then indicated the bonfire.

"That's quite an edifice you're constructing there."

"Aye," Magnuss agreed doubtfully. "Not as high as I would like, but the best we can do in a wooded valley."

"You'll be dancing round it?"

He nodded.

"*Helt sikkert*; for certain, Sister! Where I come from, we believe that like All Hallow's, the veil between the worlds is thinned on Midsummer's Eve.

"Whilst we celebrate life and the warmth of the sun, the fires will ward off any dragons or adventurous faery spirits who may be wandering in our midst."

Ursula smiled.

"Well, we at Langlois ignite our fires to symbolise Saint John, who foretold the coming of our Lord and therefore light, into this world. Though I'd like to dance round your bonfire and help keep those faeries at bay, I'll be content to gather herbs that night as is tradition, and observe the flames from a distance."

Estrid, when Ursula paid her a visit at the constable's cottage, said she'd be doing much the same.

"There'll be no dancing for me this year with this blessed ankle!"

"Never mind," Ursula soothed. "That Viking husband of yours will scare off any dragons.

"Now, let's see how that swelling is, shall we?"

No visit to the manor would be complete without a word with Lady Constantina who, with her brother Lord Alain, kept Becenan safe and prosperous, and was Ursula's particular friend.

Outwardly so different in appearance, the two women had much in common, including a dry wit. The lady was waiting with a cooling drink when Ursula returned to the bailey, elegant and fresh in a butter-yellow girdled gown.

"You've brought the sunshine with you, I see," she greeted the nun.

"And you look like it," Ursula countered, smiling. "I envy you that light veil."

Constantina led her friend to a shaded nook against one wall.

"Well, at least let me cool you down with a drink. Now, tell me, what news from the woods?"

Ursula recounted the details of her travelling patients, confiding her suspicions of both young men. Constantina's fine brows met.

"They may be a little mysterious, but not every traveller is a trusting soul. The road can be a dangerous place at times. And you do have a rather . . . active mind, my dear."

Ursula grimaced, recalling past mysteries she'd been involved with.

"I do indeed," she agreed ruefully.

✳   ✳   ✳   ✳

Suspicious mind aside, Ursula wasn't surprised to find the mysterious Master Laisney approaching her apprentice in Langlois's walled garden, in a perfect imitation of hunter stalking fawn.

That the shy novice had piqued his interest was obvious; less so was Bridget's reaction to it.

Home And Away

I love it when my friends turn up, arriving for a stay,
I love to see my family, who live so far away.
And when an invitation comes to pay a visit back,
I'm glad to get my ticket booked, and head upstairs to pack.
It's great to be so welcomed in, no need to rush and go,
To fill a leisured cuppa up and drink it nice and slow.
Such happy times I spend away, with those I love the best,
To sit and chat for hours and hours — or simply sit and rest.
Yet when the time has come to leave, though sad, it must be said,
There's nothing like returning home to one's own comfy bed!

Maggie Ingall

Thanks to abusive relatives in her past, she usually always avoided men. But this was a young one, slim and personable.

Ursula paused in the shadows, ready to intervene, as Bridget turned and saw Laisney. He froze, extending a reassuring hand.

"'Tis all right," he said. "I mean you no harm. I just came to see if I could help."

He gestured to the trug of herbs she was gathering. Bridget remained poised for flight, eyes wide and watchful, as he knelt a little distance from her.

"Can you show me what to collect?"

Ursula held her breath, wondering how her little chick would react. But she was not destined to know, for just then, a terrific cry split the air and she whirled to rush to the infirmary as fast as her legs would allow.

There, her fallen angel was tearing his bedding apart as he hunted for something.

"Whatever's the matter?" she cried, hurrying over.

"My talisman!" Segar sobbed, his chest heaving with hard, shallow breaths. "It's gone!"

"It cannot be far." Ursula took hold of his flailing arms and propelled him towards the fireside. "Now, sit, breathe and let me look. You'll wear yourself to cinders with all this fuss."

But Segar would not settle, his lamentations made worse by the arrival of Lady Edith.

"This is outrageous!" she screeched, reminding Ursula of the crows that squabbled and circled round the convent walls. "That pendant is extremely valuable. I insist a full search be made immediately!"

"Calm yourself, Madame," Ursula bade her. "We will of course look . . ."

"This is your fault!" Edith whirled on the little nun with a pointed, talon-like finger. "You should never have left my son alone."

Before she could allow temper to overcome judgement, Segar was sighing.

"Mother, please!"

"Hush, now," Ursula soothed, reaching for his hand, feeling it tremble and frowning. "There's naught to fear. We'll find your pendant and, in return, you will take your medicine and return to bed."

Ignoring Edith's outraged snorts, Ursula led him to a vacant cot and gently but firmly tucked him under the blankets.

Bridget, waiting in the wings, came forward at Ursula's command to be sent with instructions for a search to be made for the missing pendant. To her relief, Ursula watched Lady Edith stalk out after the novice.

She hurriedly mixed another soothing tincture for the anxious Segar.

"I must have that talisman," he murmured.

"There is no hurry," she said, sitting beside him as he drank. "You are protected under this roof."

The eyes that met hers were so sorrowful, her heart twisted.

"And beyond that?"

Ursula took his hand with the stalwartness for which she was renowned.

"Well, there's always your mother. It would be a brave or very foolish soul who'd take her on!"

She was rewarded with a grin as Segar chuckled and squeezed her fingers.

Ursula waited until he was sound asleep and Bridget back to watch over him before she left the infirmary for the private lodgings of Prioress Osyth. Langlois's leader was noble, wise and well respected, qualities which Ursula felt in need of now.

Osyth's ready smile for her infirmarian held a trace of pique.

"Let me guess," Ursula said grimly. "You've been visited by Edith Velyn, crying theft."

"Shrieking is more accurate," Osyth corrected, waving Ursula to the stool opposite hers across the desk. "Apparently, Langlois is a hotbed of vice and I a queen of mismanagement, who allows her nuns to run around the valley when they should be caring for others."

She was startled into laughter by the angry flush on Ursula's merry countenance.

"My dear, you look like a pot about to boil over! Simmer down, and tell me what's really going on with these guests."

Uncurling her fingers, Ursula tucked them into their habitual pose within her wide sleeves and told Osyth of the Velyns and the Glain Nedre jewel.

"He worries me," she confessed. "'Tis the point of the pendant I sense concerns him most, not its cost."

"You mean, he feels in need of protection?"

"He is burdened by something."

Osyth was rubbing a ruminative finger across her chin.

"Mayhap that's the real reason behind their pilgrimage."

"Whatever it is, it's making him ill," Ursula concluded. "And I fear if I cannot lessen his symptoms, he may not make it to Lindisfarne at all."

"Then," Osyth said firmly, "you must work your particular magic and see if he will trust you with the truth."

Though flattered by Osyth's faith in her abilities, Ursula's brows were bent as she descended the steps from the prioress's lodgings and began to cross the court, head lowered and hands in sleeves.

Curiosity was her besetting sin, and she must guard against indulging it to the detriment of her patient's care.

But if she was right, and whatever hounded Segar was hindering his recovery, it was her duty to do what she could to help. She hadn't mentioned her suspicions of Ahren Laisney to Osyth.

That was unlike her, and she wondered why. Oh, well, no time to dwell on it. There was work to do.

She was brought up short at the infirmary entrance by the sight of indents in the patch of grass there. One clear mark showed someone had stood in the earth, for some while at least, as if waiting for something.

She pondered over it whilst conducting a thorough if necessarily hushed search of the infirmary, so as not to disturb sleeping patients. No talisman.

Moving on to her stillroom, she clucked her tongue at the discovery of dust hugging her less popular medicine jars, and set to work erasing all traces of it from her shelves.

It was clear now that the talisman had been taken, probably during the brief period when both Ursula and Bridget were absent from here.

Why was another question. Had someone recognised the value of the pendant? Perhaps. But Ursula had a hunch that something else lay behind the disappearance.

Lady Edith cared naught for the why, only the where, and when the search was paused for the nuns to attend Sext service, rudely demanded some miss their devotions until the jewel was found.

"My husband was friends with a bishop, and he shall hear of this! A hideaway for pickpockets, this place is!"

Before certain outraged nuns, Ursula among them, could react, the calming voice of the prioress washed over them.

"You are wearing yourself out with worry, my lady. Come and rest awhile in the privacy of my chambers."

She led the bristling woman up to her lodgings, a tiny smile crossing her heart-shaped countenance at the faces of her nuns left behind.

* * * *

The sun's warmth was so pleasant, Ursula coaxed Segar out into her cloister-walk paradyse garden, where the calming sound of fountain water was framed by a rainbow of flowers.

"Keep me company whilst I weed."

Sighing, he tipped his face to the sun, momentarily content before his features clouded again.

"I must apologise for my mother," he began. "She can never forget her station, sometimes at the expense of her manners."

"In this instance," Ursula ventured, teasing out the good-for-nothings from her flowered gems, "I believe she's acting on your behalf. She knows how you value that talisman. As do I."

"And you wonder why," Segar murmured after a pause.

Ursula shrugged.

"I just want you to get to your shrine, seek your absolution for that burden you carry."

Segar leaned forward.

"May I confide in you, Sister?"

"I am not a confessor," Ursula reminded him, "and it is God who will judge you."

"I know, but I would have you know the truth about me. You're right in your assumption that it's for me, not my father, that we go on pilgrimage.

"You see, I killed a girl. I didn't mean to," he added hastily. "I cared for her! But she was . . . unsuitable."

"And your mother put a stop to the liaison," Ursula guessed.

Segar nodded.

"I was too weak to make more than a token protest. Truth be told, my feelings weren't strong enough to fight Mother's logic. But Alana, the girl, she took it badly, accused me of betrayal and cowardice.

"And she was right." He sighed. "I wanted to make amends. But I never got the chance.

"She took her own life before I could do anything.

"Her family vowed revenge. What they didn't realise is that they already have it. She haunts me, Sister."

Ursula reached to take his hand.

"Put your faith in a Higher Being," she advised. "There will be a way to right this unintended wrong."

His smile was grateful.

"You encourage me to hope," he murmured.

Ursula squeezed his fingers, then leaned on him for help to rise from her knees.

"I will restore your talisman, too," she promised. "A little extra protection never hurts!"

It was difficult not to be distracted by the sight of her little chick being cosseted by a young man who, by dint of gentle patience, had persuaded Bridget to allow him close enough to help her with laying out the infirmary's washing to dry.

Ahren Laisney's manner spoke of a kindness that said much for him. But there was another young man who also had value, and deserved a second chance.

Bridget smiled as her mentor approached, accepting the change of duties back to the infirmary with her usual shy obedience.

Ahren's own smile was somewhat hesitant as Ursula took Bridget's place.

"Well, Master Laisney, you are making yourself useful."

When he shrugged, she narrowed her eyes at him.

"It's time you were frank with me. What is your real reason for being here? And why do you take such pains with my apprentice?"

The flush that had risen in his neck deepened.

"I mean Bridget no harm! 'Tis just that . . ."

"She reminds you of another," Ursula finished as enlightenment dawned.

Eyes flaring, Ahren nodded.

"My sister, as close to me as a twin. Bridget is so like Alana, so vulnerable . . ."

"It all becomes clear now." Clucking her tongue, Ursula nudged Ahren into the shade of a fruiting pear. "You're here to take revenge on Segar Velyn."

"You know what that rogue did to her?"

"Segar has told me his side of this sorry tale, but I suspect he doesn't know the full truth."

Under her stern gaze, Ahren flushed again.

"He ruined her and broke her heart, that is true," he muttered fiercely. "But he did not kill her."

"Nay." Ahren glared at Ursula, then, subsiding, sighed. "Though as good as, in my eyes.

"Alana's future was destroyed; she could not view her life in any other way. So she gave it up, gave me up.

"She is Sister Fidelis now, hidden away in a borderlands nunnery. She's as far away from me there as if she had died."

"Fidelis," Ursula murmured. "The faithful one . . . Your sister will never be out of reach, no matter where she dwells.

"Go and see her; you might be surprised at how time in a cloistered world will have brought her some peace. Trust me, I know." For the second time that day, she patted a young man's hand.

"But first, you can search the infirmary for that talisman, which I have a feeling will be miraculously discovered. Velyn has been tormented enough."

When he stared at her, she looked pointedly back.

"A piece of advice, my son. If you're going to wait outside my infirmary for a chance to steal from a sleeping patient, do not step in earth and leave your footmarks."

Ahren's smile was sheepish.

"As you wish, Sister. I'll come back this way and, if I may, stop and help Bridget for a day or two." He rose, bowed and sauntered off across the garden.

At the gate, he turned back.

"How did you know Alana was alive?"

"You would have been out for his blood," Ursula said simply, "not just his peace of mind."

$$* \quad * \quad * \quad *$$

There was a hush in the air this Midsummer morn as dawn spread long, blush-pink fingers across the skies, the smoke from last night's fires still lingering to create a strange but pleasant mist.

Ursula breathed in deeply as she made her way to the church for the first of three masses to celebrate the Feast of St John.

If any faery spirits had been abroad last night, she was sure Magnuss and company had kept them at bay, recalling the sight of dancing fires in the valley below the wooded ridge that she and Bridget had glimpsed whilst gathering mallow, rue, foxgloves and, of course, St John's wort, by the light of their own little flame.

The pilgrims had been invited to share in the celebrations, and much to Ursula's delight, she'd spied Segar and Ahren with their heads together, Segar ignoring his mother's gripes for once as they tried to find something positive out of past faults.

Already, her haunted patient was showing signs of renewed life, a natural bloom slowly returning to his skin.

Ursula had high hopes that between them, these two young souls could find peace, as would the girl that they both loved in such different ways.

And wasn't that exactly as it should be on this, the day that celebrated the saint who brought the world its biggest hope of all?

A touch on her arm revealed Bridget standing beside her.

Was it just her fancy, or did her young apprentice seem to have a little more assurance about her? If so, it was yet another thing to be thankful for.

Smiling, Ursula tucked her arm through Bridget's.

"Come, chick," she said. "It's time to celebrate . . ." ∎

Fishguard, Pembrokeshire

Centuries ago, when Viking invaders routinely landed on the British Isles, a small village on Wales's south-western shores acquired a very un-Welsh sounding name. Its Welsh name of Abergwaun ("Mouth of the River Gwaun") described its location. Its new name, Fiskigarðr, was Old Norse for "fish catching enclosure".

That we now know the town as Fishguard, a beautiful and popular tourist destination, suggests the Vikings had a role in its history.

The town was also the focus of what became known as the last invasion in Britain. In February 1797, 1,400 French soldiers landed at Carreg Wastad, some five miles away. Legend has it that Jemima Nicholas, armed only with a pitchfork, single-handedly captured 12 French invaders and secured them in St Mary's Church.

Today, the event is commemorated in the award-winning Last Invasion Tapestry. Designed on the model of the Bayeux Tapestry and commissioned by the Fishguard Arts Society for the bicentennial of the surrender, it took 77 local embroiderers four years to make and is on display in the town hall library.

A Helping Hand

by Liz Filleul

WALKING out with that constable again, I suppose!" Mrs Ellis sniffed disapproval as Bess paused at the back door to wrap her black shawl around her skinny shoulders. "I've said it before and I'll say it again. No good will come of it." The cook slammed her metal ladle against the side of the copper pot that hung over the fire.

Bess didn't answer. There was no point defending her relationship with Constable Jem Welbeck. Mrs Ellis was of the firm belief that young maids — especially young convict maids — shouldn't spend their Sunday afternoons courting.

Even if Sunday afternoon was the only free time Bess had.

Bess opened the back door and shivered at the icy blast. It was a shame to have to leave the cosy kitchen. Her thin shawl and convict shift offered no protection from the Van Diemen's Land winter.

But the thought of Jem waiting for her by the Hobart Town rivulet warmed her heart.

"I shan't be late, Mrs Ellis," she promised as she stepped outside.

"You'd better not be," the cook responded. "And don't you do anything you shouldn't, you hear me? You don't want to find yourself back in Cascades!"

Cascades Female Factory was the Hobart Town gaol Bess had been taken to when she'd first been transported. She'd spent one night there before being assigned to free settlers to work off part of her sentence as an unpaid maid.

A Ticket of Leave after three years was a more enticing prospect than spending her full six-year sentence in the fortress-like gaol. But Bess had soon discovered that she would work hard for that ticket.

Mrs Ellis did the cooking, but Bess did all the cleaning and laundry. She worked from five-thirty each morning till sometimes late at night.

But Mr and Mrs Fayne, while cold and distant, didn't ill-treat her. Bess

Illustration by David Young.

even had her own tiny bedroom next to the kitchen. And while Mrs Ellis might have a sharp tongue, she made sure Bess had plenty to eat.

"I'm not going to be doing anything I shouldn't when I'm with a constable, now, am I?" Bess called now to Mrs Ellis, closing the door quickly so she didn't have to hear her response.

It was a clear day, despite the biting cold. The Faynes' property had a magnificent view over Sullivan's Cove, which today was a sparkling blue and busy with whalers and trading ships.

Bess walked briskly down the hill, along Macquarie Street with its elegant sandstone government buildings, and then headed down Elizabeth Street, towards the rivulet.

Two years ago, if anyone had told her she'd fall in love with a policeman – or "trap", as they were called in Van Diemen's Land – she'd have laughed at them, Bess reflected as she strode past the closed shops.

She'd seen police as the enemy in England, when she'd taken to stealing to stave off hunger or pay for shelter on a rainy night.

They were the enemy in Hobart Town, too, especially those traitorous convict constables, who'd agreed to join the police force in exchange for an early Ticket of Leave.

It was the constables who usually captured convict maids who'd run away from their masters. The constables didn't care if the maid had been beaten or starved – all they cared about was the extra sovereign they earned for catching a bolter.

It was the constables, too, who, if they caught convict maids drinking or dancing in the taverns, offered to turn a blind eye in return for certain favours.

Bess would normally trust a red-coated British soldier more than a constable.

But then, two months ago, she'd met Jem.

*   *   *   *

She'd been on her way home, struggling with two full pails of water, after a trip to the water storage tower in Macquarie Street.

In one way, Bess always looked forward to collecting water. It offered a chance to chat with other convict maids.

But gossip was always followed by the painful struggle through Hobart Town's rough and hilly streets, feeling like her arms were being wrenched from their sockets as she tried not to spill a precious drop.

That day, she'd caught her foot in a hole, stumbled and crashed to the ground. Her pails had gone airborne, sloshing water over the road.

Bess cursed aloud. Now she'd have to refill them.

"Are you hurt?"

The tone was gentle, at odds with the police uniform that was the first thing Bess noticed as she clambered to her feet. The second thing she noticed was that there was no red badge on the uniform, meaning this was a free-settler policeman.

The final thing she noticed was how handsome he was. Red-haired, chiselled cheek bones, a shy smile.

She felt heat rise in her cheeks and looked away quickly.

"I'm fine," she muttered, "thank you."

She wasn't, though. Her hands and knees were badly scraped and smeared with dirt. She'd torn a hole in her shift as well; she'd have to mend it later.

The constable retrieved the rolling pails.

"How far are you from your master's house?"

Bess pointed.

"Just up the hill."

"A fair walk and your hands look sore. Come on, I'll help you fill them, and carry them back for you."

Part of Bess cringed at the idea of her friends seeing her with a policeman. Especially if he was carrying her pails! She'd never live it down.

But part of her was glad of his help.

They began walking in the direction of Macquarie Street.

"How long have you been out here?" he asked her in a chummy tone.

"Two years," Bess answered. "I get my Ticket of Leave next year."

"That's good. Any plans for when you've got it?"

"Not yet, no."

Bess was worried about that. There wasn't much work in the colony for Ticket-of-Leave women — especially those like Bess, who couldn't read or write or cook or sew or do anything that was useful to the free settlers.

She could scrub clothes and clean houses, but no free settler would pay for that when they could get free labour from Cascades.

"You've got time to think about it," he said.

Bess rolled her eyes. She wouldn't acquire any skills over the next twelve months as a convict maid.

"What about you?" she asked. "How long have you been out here?"

"Five years. Me and my brother came out, thinking there'd be more opportunities here than in England."

"And are there?"

He shrugged.

"We've both got work. Simon's at the sawmill and I've got this job. We have roofs over our heads and we can afford to eat." He glanced at her curiously. "What did you do to be transported?"

"I stole some candlesticks," she admitted. "Smashed a shop window and grabbed them to pawn. I'd already tied the shop door so the shopkeeper couldn't come after me.

"But I ran right into a policeman. It wasn't the first time I'd been caught thieving, so transportation it was." She glanced at him to gauge his reaction.

"You don't look disgusted."

"I'm not," he said. "In truth, if me and Simon hadn't come out here, we might have ended up transported, too."

After Jem had carried the pails back to the Faynes', he made another offer.

"Do you have Sunday afternoons off like most convict maids?"

"I do," she answered.

"Well, maybe we could meet. Go for a walk, perhaps?"

As a free settler, he could walk out with whoever he liked.

"All right," she said. "Where do you want to meet?"

Their meeting place was by the corn mill, on the track that ran beside the stream known as the Hobart Rivulet. Bess had got used to the teasing of the other convict maids after she and Jem had been spotted together.

Mostly, the teasing was good-natured, but not always.

"A traitor to all of us you are, setting your cap at a trap."

"You know traps don't earn much, don't you? And they live in wooden huts!"

"He won't marry you, Bess, you're too plain. A handsome free settler like him can have any pretty girl he wants."

Bess ignored their remarks, like she ignored Mrs Ellis. It didn't matter to her that Jem was poor – he was kind, the only man in her twenty-one years to genuinely care about her.

And yes, she was skinny and mousy-haired, but if looks were all he cared about, he wouldn't have invited her to walk out with him in the first place.

After two months she was convinced she had a future with Jem – even if it was living in a little wooden hut behind the police office.

She'd slept in worse places.

But now, as she approached the rivulet, she saw something that made her wonder whether the other convict maids and Mrs Ellis might be right.

Jem was standing on the track talking to a woman around Bess's own age. She had long auburn hair and wore a fashionable pale blue conical skirt.

They were laughing together, and when they saw Bess, the woman said something to Jem. He nodded to her and she walked away in the direction of the wharves.

Bess felt like her heart had fallen into her boots. Why had she believed Jem would prefer a plain convict maid like her to a beautiful free settler like the auburn-haired woman?

Had Bess been just a diversion till someone better came along?

"Afternoon, Bess," Jem said as she joined him. As usual, he wore his constable's uniform, because the police always had to be dressed for an emergency.

"I can't walk for long today. I'm on an earlier watch tonight."

Bess didn't believe him. He was slipping away early to meet the auburn-haired woman, she was sure of it.

"Who was that woman you were talking to just now?" she asked, unable to keep her voice steady.

"Oh, that was Norah." Jem took her arm and steered her along the track in the opposite direction from the wharves.

"She's walking out with Constable Grafton. She just got her Ticket of Leave and has taken up sewing for the grand ladies here. She was just telling me she made that skirt from some leftover material."

"I've never seen her at the water storage tower."

"She was assigned to a family on the edge of town, never came in."

Bess didn't know whether to believe him or not, so was quiet for most of their walk. The rivulet was peaceful, especially with the mills and brewery closed on Sundays.

The only sounds were the gurgle of the mud-coloured rivulet, the warbling of magpies and laughter of kookaburras, and the footfalls and murmured conversations of other couples taking an afternoon stroll.

"You're not upset about Norah, are you?" Jem asked later, when they parted outside the Macquarie Street police office. "There's no need to be. Ask anyone here who she's walking out with and they'll tell you it's Will Grafton. Meet you same time next Sunday?"

"Yes," Bess agreed.

But still, she was worried.

I can't make myself pretty like Norah but I need to make myself useful somehow, Bess thought as she walked back to the Faynes'.

Bess was still pondering what she could do to make herself more useful a couple of days later when she was queuing at the water storage tower.

The gossip today was that Kitty, who'd been transported on the same

Autumn Poem

Summer is fading fast
As God quietly rolls away
The glorious span of sunshine
That warmed my heart today.

Cool evenings tap my shoulder
As if somehow to say
Autumn is gently waiting,
Time to wave summer away.

I'll miss her golden heartbeat
In that early morning call,
As birds chorus and chatter
And summer wakes us all.

Yet autumn is the season
Of both renewal and rest.
I glow with silent gratitude;
We've yet to see her best.

As summer bows to autumn
And crowns her next to reign,
I can see the glorious hand
Of God at work again.

Karen Taylor

ship as Bess, was back in Cascades. She'd bolted with a Ticket-of-Leave man and they'd been caught by the traps.

"I wish I was back in Cascades," a voice behind Bess said.

She turned around. The speaker was smaller than Bess, and a bruise stained her pale face. Her shift was clean, indicating she'd only recently been transported.

"Cascades is terrible," Bess told her. "They shave your hair off and make you stand outside at the sinks all day scrubbing laundry from the men's gaol."

The girl shrugged.

"Better than being with my master. He treats me like a slave."

"Run away, then," Jane, in front of Bess, suggested. "You'll get caught by the traps, and be put in Cascades for six months, like Bess says. But then they'll send you to a different master. They're not all bad. You might get a better one next time."

A tear rolled down the girl's face. Bess felt sorry for her. The girl wouldn't survive five minutes on the run. And some of the traps could be rough.

But what was she thinking? Here was a chance for Bess to help the girl – and to prove her worth to Jem as well! Show him she was useful!

"Do you get Sunday afternoons off?" she whispered. "I've got an idea."

* * * *

Bess hurried down Elizabeth Street, relieved that Sunday afternoon had finally arrived. It seemed an eternity since she'd hatched her plan with the convict maid, Mary.

Jem stood waiting by the corn mill. He waved as she approached.

"Afternoon, Bess."

"Afternoon, Jem."

He took her arm and they began their walk. Bess's heart was pounding as they rounded a corner and she spotted Mary, in tell-tale black shawl, white shift and mob cap, crouched behind a fern.

Mary, as agreed, took to her heels when Bess and Jem appeared.

"Why, that looks like the bolter we've been told to keep an eye out for! Excuse me, Bess."

Jem sprinted along the track, easily catching up with Mary. He snapped a handcuff around her wrist.

"I'll have to take her to the cells," he told Bess apologetically.

"Wait a minute, Jem." Bess held up her hand. "I've made an agreement with Mary here."

"An agreement?" Jem frowned. "What d'you mean?"

"Mary's master was beating her and she wanted to go back to Cascades," Bess told him. "So I agreed with her that she should bolt and hide where you'd find her.

"That way you'll get a sovereign for catching a bolter – but you have to give half of it to her when she comes out of Cascades."

Bess had been proud of her plan. She'd envisaged being able to help other unhappy maids in this way.

She'd assumed Jem would like her plan, too. A way of helping people and earning extra money.

But Jem didn't look happy. He glowered at her.

"I'm a policeman! I'm not doing anything corrupt!"

"But the police are corrupt," Bess reminded him.

"Well, I'm not. I do an honest day's work and I don't want to jeopardise my job. I'll have to take her to the cells but I don't want a penny of that sovereign."

Bess fled. She ran away from the rivulet, all the way back to the Faynes'. She stumbled into the kitchen, breathless and crying.

"Lawks," Mrs Ellis said. "Whatever's the matter? Your young

constable, I'm guessing? Didn't I say it wouldn't end well?"

Bess hurried to her tiny bedroom, closing the door before flinging herself on the bed.

She'd ruined everything. Jem now thought she was just a dishonest convict maid who'd tried to involve him in a crooked scheme.

He'd want nothing more to do with her.

"No use shutting yourself in there crying," Mrs Ellis called. "Come and have some tea and a slice of seed cake."

Bess sighed and rose from the bed. There'd be no peace until she gave in.

A bang on the back door startled Mrs Ellis as she poured tea into a metal mug.

"See who that is, Bess."

Bess scrubbed tears from her face before opening the door. Her insides clenched. Jem looked down at her.

"Why did you run away?" he asked. "I'd have come after you, only I had to take Mary to the cells."

Bess stepped outside, closing the door behind her.

"I thought you'd want nothing more to do with me."

"Why would you think that?"

"Because of what I did."

Jem shrugged.

"You meant well. You intended me and Mary to split the sovereign between us. You wanted nothing for yourself, which shows what an unselfish girl you are."

"I just wanted to show you I was useful," Bess burst out.

"Useful?"

"I can't sew like Norah, or cook like Mrs Ellis, and I can't read or write. All I can do is scrub and clean."

He smiled.

"Well, I don't have many skills, either. I never was much good at learning. That's why I ended up a constable. It was the only job I could get. But I want to do the job well, build a good life here. And I want that life to include you."

He planned a future for them! Bess felt like crying again, she was so relieved.

"What happened about that sovereign?"

"I'll keep it for Mary. But next time you meet a maid who's not being treated right, tell me. I might be able to help in a way that doesn't involve her having to be sent back to Cascades."

The door opened behind them.

"Are you two going to stand in the cold all afternoon when there's a fire in here and tea and seed cake on the table?" Mrs Ellis demanded.

Jem grinned.

"Shall we go in?"

Bess nodded and as they stepped inside, Mrs Ellis drew her aside and whispered to her.

"You could do worse, Bess, you could do worse." ∎

Bargain

Hunt

Debut Author

by Sally Winterflood

I 'M looking across the field at the bunting on the cream teas
marquee, and all the little gingham triangles are flapping vigorously
in the gathering breeze.

"That wind's definitely picking up. I hope it doesn't rain."

Sue, my long-standing friend and trusty helper on the Good As New
clothing stall, grunts her agreement.

Bent double, she's struggling to disentangle a trouser hanger from the
large bagful that's been stored up in my attic since last year's summer
fête.

With a triumphant, "Yes!" she wiggles it free, and slips a pair of beige
ladies' trousers over the bar. Glancing across at the bunting
apprehensively, she nods.

"You're right, Jan, fingers crossed."

We carry on working our way through the bags of last-minute
donations. Luckily there aren't too many, as most of our stock was
dropped off to my house last week.

Sue and I spent all day Thursday separating the wheat from the chaff,
as my mum would have said, and deciding on pricing. It was quite a
task, as the term "good as new" isn't always entirely accurate.

Some of the stuff's pretty tatty, to be brutally honest, but we've a fair
selection of good stuff, too, and even some unworn items, still with
labels on.

It takes a while to get everything ready, but we don't mind giving up
our time once a year. It's just what you do, isn't it? Part of village life,
and all that.

We're always worn out by the end of the day, but we enjoy doing it.
The profits all go towards the upkeep of St Peter's, and although neither
of us are what you'd exactly call regulars, it's a lovely old church, and
the Rev's a good guy.

Apparently, this year we're raising funds to go towards installing a

brand-new loo – fancy!

Our fête's quite traditional. Almost old-fashioned, you might say. Apart from the inevitable bouncy castle for the kids, it's all the usual stuff, tombola, bric-à-brac, cream teas and of course, our stall.

Anyway, it's nearly two. Only five minutes till the fête officially opens. There's a cluster of about 30 people hovering over by the gate.

I can spot a few familiar faces, but East Levinton's a large village, and although I've lived here for eight years, I certainly don't know everyone.

We also get a few non-locals who come, hopeful of finding designer labels at ridiculously cheap prices.

The skinny ones get lucky, as we've several wealthy, stick-thin fashionistas in the village who regularly donate their cast-offs once they're no longer what they call "on trend".

Who dreamed up that daft phrase? What's wrong with "in fashion"? Or am I showing my age now?

I see the Rev's holding the roving mic now, ready to welcome everyone, and the gate's being opened. There's a surge of women heading our way. Always happens. They make a bee-line for our bargains.

I take a quick swig from my water bottle and brace myself.

"Ready, Sue?"

"As I'll ever be."

"Good grief, look, some of them are actually running."

"Here we go then." Sue winks at me and grins. "Let battle commence."

We're both flat out for 20 minutes, stuffing clothes into carrier bags, totting up as we go, taking money and giving change.

Inevitably there are always people who proffer twenty-pound notes for something only costing a fiver, and Sue's got one now. Struggling to serve two people at once, she calls over to me.

"Can you do a ten and two fives for a twenty?"

"Sure." I delve into my cash bag, and we exchange notes, along with wry smiles.

* * * *

Only another hour left, and the stand's starting to look a mess now. It amazes me every year, just how rapidly our orderly hanging rails come to resemble the last day of the sales.

Within minutes, there are clothes on the floor, skew-whiff on their hangers, and some are flung carelessly over the top of the rails like old rags.

And as for the jumble of tops and jumpers on the trestle tables – we might just as well have left everything in one big heap, not bothered folding them neatly, M&S-style, after all.

But it does mean we're selling lots, which is great, as we're always on a mission to up our takings, year on year.

How much does it cost to install a loo in a church anyway, I wonder?

Now that the initial scrum is over, we only have two people looking around the stall.

"I'll have a quick tidy-up, as it's calmed down," I say to Sue, who's already begun to gather up the empty hangers that we flung beneath the tables during the rush.

"Good idea." She grins at me. "I'll nip over to the cider stand in a bit and get us a couple of halves."

A woman I vaguely recognise, but don't actually know, has just begun flicking speedily through the rail of jackets. She's about my age, I'd say, well dressed, and probably not short of a bob or two, judging by the Gucci logo on her leather bag.

She has a rather harassed air about her, and she's shunting hangers aside so forcefully that the scrape of metal on metal is setting my teeth on edge.

Everything's getting squashed tight together, too. I can't help feeling a bit irritated by her treatment of our "stock".

She's stopped to pull one out for a better look. Ah, it's the one I tried that was too tight on the shoulders. Great choice.

Classic cream linen, brand new, unworn, label still on, it's an absolute steal at ten pounds.

"Nice jacket, isn't it?" I say, as I catch her eye and smile. "Never been worn."

The woman doesn't return the smile, but makes a non-committal sort of face. Undaunted, I fetch the mirror, and hold it up in front of her as she slips it on. It fits her perfectly.

"Looks lovely on you." I flash my encouraging, shop-assistant smile at her.

She gives me a withering look, but says nothing as she turns sideways-on to the mirror, then shimmies out of the jacket and examines our hand-written price label, hanging alongside the original one.

"Well, I wouldn't pay that for it," she says sniffily at last. "It's second-hand, you can't charge ten pounds. I'll give you five."

"It's never been worn," I counter. "Still got its label on." I pull forward the shop's tag to show her. "See? It was eighty-five pounds. I'd say that makes this a real bargain."

Resolute, she shakes her head.

"Five pounds. It's nearly the end of the fête anyway, and you're unlikely to sell it now. You'll only be stuck with it."

"The money's not going in my pocket, you know!" I snap at her. "It's for St Peter's."

I probably shouldn't have said that, but I couldn't help myself, and she can clearly afford it. So I fix her with what my daughter calls "the look", hold my ground, and remain silent.

I'm blowed if she's going to have it for five pounds. There's a principle involved here.

"Well, you've just lost yourself a sale, then." And with that, she thrusts the offending jacket at me and stalks off in the direction of the bric-à-brac stall.

Sue scurries over.

"Well done, Jan! What a nerve! You know who she is, don't you?"

"No. She's familiar, but I don't know her."

"She's Gladys's daughter-in-law."

"Gladys from the WI?"

"Yup. Hermione Lawson; she's married to Gladys's son, Marcus – got two daughters, apparently. They bought Mallards, that big place at the end of Pond Lane, about six months ago."

"Definitely not short of money then," I observe. "But Gladys is such a sweetie. How can she be related to someone like that?"

Sue rolls her eyes at me.

"Like I said, daughter-in-law, not daughter."

It's quarter to five now, the brass band are packing up their instruments, and everything's winding down. We've had a good day, and it didn't rain.

"Hello, dear." A voice behind me makes me jump. "Wonderful fete, as always."

It's Gladys. I suddenly feel embarrassed about my confrontation with her daughter-in-law. I'm sure I'm blushing.

"Gladys. Nice to see you. Are you well?"

"Yes, thank you dear. Getting excited now, of course."

I've no clue what she's referring to.

"Oh? Why? What's happening?"

"Haven't I told you? My granddaughter Phoebe's getting married soon. Two weeks today, in fact. Here at St Peter's."

"I'd no idea. How lovely."

Sue is bearing two plastic glasses, glowing temptingly golden in the late afternoon sunshine.

She hesitates, unsure about passing one to me while I'm serving, so to speak.

"Don't mind me," Gladys insists. "Go ahead, enjoy your drinks, you two. You've certainly earned them."

The cider slips down easily. Crisp, not overly sweet, it tastes deliciously of ripe apples and autumn harvest. My feet are beginning to ache, so I perch on the edge of one of our tables.

"Let's hope you have a beautiful, sunny day for the wedding, Gladys."

She flashes me an optimistic smile.

"Fingers crossed, dear. The reception's at Mallards; a big marquee in the garden, so we don't want rain, that's for sure."

"No, indeed."

"Actually, I'm looking for something suitable to wear with the new dress I've bought. Just in case, heaven forbid, it rains, or gets chilly in the evening.

"I'm afraid I feel the cold more now that I'm getting older."

"What's your dress like?" I say, as I drain my glass and amble over to stand beside her. "What colour is it?"

"It's floral, so pretty, all the colours of a summer garden, three-quarter length sleeves and just below the knee.

"I'm so pleased with it, but I need something. Not a cardigan, that's not dressy enough – a little jacket, perhaps."

"How about this one?" I say, as I pull it off the rail. "It looks about your size, and being cream, it'll work well."

I hold up the mirror and have a moment's déjà-vu.

"Looks lovely on you."

Gladys beams, first at her own reflection, then at me.

"It's perfect. How clever of you." She slips it off, looks at the two price tags, and frowns.

"Oh, I can't pay that for it."

My heart sinks.

"No," she says firmly, pulling out her purse, "it's obvious it's never been worn, and look at what it cost brand new! I couldn't possibly only give you ten pounds, not when the proceeds are going to St Peter's. I insist on giving you twenty."

Moved, I can only manage a small smile.

"Thank you, Gladys, that's so generous of you."

"Nonsense," she says with a little grin. "It's still a great bargain. And we need another toilet in the church. Reverend Spencer's sermons can be very long sometimes, believe me!"

As I'm folding the jacket, ready to put into a bag, an idea pops into my head.

"We have a few little silky scarves left over – would you like one? No charge. As a thank-you for your generosity?"

"That's very kind of you, dear, but I don't really wear them. Too fussy for me.

"Although, perhaps . . . would you mind if I chose one for my daughter-in-law instead? She loves scarves."

Sue looks over at me, boggle-eyed, clearly amused at this turn of events. I simply smile my most benevolent smile.

"Of course we don't mind, Gladys. Choose two if you like – our pleasure." ■

Shutterstock.

Plas Newydd

Plas Newydd is an 18th-century mansion house designed by architect James Wyatt, who made changes to the original Tudor building.

The ancestral family home of the Marquess of Anglesey still has parts dating back to the 16th century and houses a huge commissioned mural, 58 feet in length, painted by Rex Whistler, one of the last extensive masterpieces by the artist before he was tragically killed in action in World War II.

Other spectacular artwork worth seeing includes Van Dyck's portrait of Katherine Manners, Duchess of Buckingham, the "richest girl in England".

Plas Newydd – or new mansion – is surrounded by beautiful gardens set on the bank of the Menai Strait with fabulous views of Snowdonia.

The deciduous woodland is home to an assortment of wildlife, and the red squirrel, once at serious risk, is now said to be thriving thanks to a reintroduction programme by the Anglesey Red Squirrel Project.

A house has sat on this prime site since the 16th century and has seen many changes over the years, including being used as a Naval cadet training base.

A Sixpenny Posy

―――― by Rosemary Gemmell ――――

T HE painting of the flower-filled cottage garden took pride of place at the art exhibition, its delicate shades of lilacs, pinks, blues and whites interspersed with red roses and yellow foxgloves.

A bird-bath stood in the centre, surrounded by small beds of fragrant herbs and yellow and orange nasturtium. Rosie sighed with pleasure, the sight of it taking her right back to her childhood and the enchanted garden.

*　*　*　*

"Run across and get me a bunch of flowers for the cemetery, Rosie."

Eight-year-old Rosie grasped the sixpenny coin, and dashed down the stairs and across the road. It was her favourite time of the week, visiting the enchanted garden.

She'd never seen so many beautiful flowers and it was the most magical place ever. She lived in an old tenement flat with Mam, Dad and two brothers and there was scarcely room for them, never mind anywhere to grow flowers.

The back green was for hanging out washing, with an enclosed area to the side for the midden bins.

Sometimes, she played out the back or held concerts with her friends, but the only flowers were weeds and thistles. So, when it was a Sunday for visiting the cemetery, Rosie made sure she was the one to get the flowers.

Mr McKenzie lived across the road in the bottom flat. But instead of a rough, weed-filled, grassy area outside the front window, his garden was enclosed in a high hedge, only hinting at the colourful treasures within.

Rosie rapped on the door and waited, hopping from one foot to the other, the small silver coin hidden in her fist.

"Hello, Rosie, lass. Come for some flowers?"

"Yes, please, Mr McKenzie. Mam and me are going up the cemetery."

He nodded, not saying a word as Rosie followed him out the close and through the gate at the side of his front garden, into another world.

No-one had much money, but they knew where to buy the best flowers for a special birthday, or the cemetery.

Mrs McKenzie was an invalid, but Rosie sometimes saw her waving from the window and Rosie always smiled and waved back.

She wished she had grandparents like them but hers were dead, which was why she and Mam went up to the cemetery so often.

"We need to remember them by putting fresh flowers on their graves, Rosie," Mam had told her.

She loved going on the bus to the big cemetery on the edge of town, where they had to walk past the ancient gravestones of long ago. Rosie hoped the grannies and grandpas liked having such pretty flowers to cheer up their graves.

Her favourite time of the year was summer, when the garden sang with masses of flowers, bees and butterflies. It was easy to forget the dull grey buildings on the dirty grey street and, instead, to smell the scents of a hundred blooms.

As always, she stood at the first path so she could drink in the sights and sounds. A bird called from one corner near the bottom and a bee buzzed right past her ear on its way to find the next drink.

Like a regiment, row upon row of flowers stood before her, of every colour and fragrance.

At first, she'd just taken the bunch of flowers Mr McKenzie had cut for her and hurried home in a daze. Now, however, they'd got used to one another, and although he still didn't talk much, Mr McKenzie was teaching her the names of the flowers, allowing her to choose which to cut.

"The lad's here today, Rosie. He'll be out in a minute. Let's have a look at what's best for you this time."

Although she was desperate to learn more names, Rosie glanced behind, hoping his grandson, Neil, was on his way. He had his own wee patch of garden away at the side and she loved to see what he'd been growing.

"Now what d'ye think of these?" He was looking at the tall stems of larkspur, lupins and foxgloves.

"I like the pretty lilac, pink and creamy ones."

"Aye, they like to show off, they do. Look at this foxglove here. What d'ye see?"

Rosie laughed. Inside one of the tiny bell-like flowers, a bee was busy sipping at the nectar.

"I think he's having a feast."

"Aye, we'll no' disturb him the now. Why don't we stroll around and see which blooms ye'd prefer today before I cut them?"

Rosie skipped along the rows, imagining a wee fairy or two might be hidden amongst the foliage of the smaller plants. She already knew the taller flowers were the only ones Mr McKenzie cut to sell.

Apart from Neil's small patch, other flower-beds at the side contained smaller plants.

"Mrs McKenzie likes her herbs and forget-me-nots," the elderly man had told her once. "And Neil likes the tom thumbs."

Rosie tried to remember the other name for the pretty yellow, orange and red tom thumbs that rambled all along the edges.

It began with N . . . nasty something, which didn't suit them at all.

Mr McKenzie saw her crouching down and stopped beside her.

"I cannae remember what else you called these tom thumbs, Mr McKenzie."

"Nasturtium. Did ye know ye can eat the petals?" He winked at her and she didn't know if he was kidding her.

"Aye, so we can." The voice came from behind and Rosie whirled round. Ten-year-old Neil grinned from beneath his sandy, floppy hair, knobbly knees visible beneath khaki shorts.

Rosie grinned back, wishing she had on her shorts instead of the flowery dress Mam made her wear on a Sunday.

"Hello, Neil. Your grandpa's cutting me some flowers." As if he didn't know that already.

"Aye. Hello, Rosie." He looked down and she wondered why his face had reddened as the sun wasn't very bright yet. Then he turned away. "Just goin' to see how my wee patch is doing."

Mr McKenzie chuckled beside her and Rosie wondered what he'd found. She brought her attention back to the rows of blooms.

"So what d'ye think of some dahlias, lass?"

Rosie thought these the showiest flowers in the garden, with their great big heads full of petals. But Mam liked them so she nodded.

"Maybe two of those with pink and yellow petals, please. Can I see the carnations and hollyhocks, and the big daisies?"

Her favourites were the large white daisies that reminded her of the daisy chains she made when playing in the park with her friends. Mam preferred the more colourful flowers, but Rosie always sneaked a big daisy or two in with them.

Rosie tried to make up her mind what to choose. She grinned at Neil when they passed him and always found him looking her way.

"Now what else will you have today, then, Rosie? Yer mam will be sending out your brothers to fetch you soon."

Since she definitely didn't want Joey or Mitch spoiling her special garden, Rosie glanced back at the other rows before deciding.

"I'd like hollyhocks, larkspur, foxgloves, dahlias and the big daisies, please."

"Aye, that's a good bunch. You hold the paper to wrap them while I cut the stems."

They were making their way to the gate from the garden when Neil came shuffling up to them, hand behind his back.

"Thought you might want a wee posy for yourself, Rosie. These are growing well an' it's good to thin them a bit."

He thrust out his hand with a shy grin.

"Oh, they're lovely. Thanks, Neil. I'll put them in a jam jar and keep them on the window-sill."

She sniffed at the lavender, rosemary and miniature pink roses, the scent filling her with pleasure.

"Here, lass, we'll wrap the stems in a bit of paper to keep your hands clean." Mr McKenzie tore off another bit of the paper.

"Thanks. Mam'll be annoyed if I get my dress dirty before we go out."

"Aye, it's a pretty frock for a pretty girl, so mind how you carry the flowers."

Rosie could hardly hold the big bunch of flowers along with the posy and had to rest it partly against her.

"Thank you, Mr McKenzie. Mam'll love these. Oh, she told me to ask how Mrs McKenzie is today."

"That's kind of her. Come and say hello as you go."

Rosie followed him to the door, Neil behind them.

"Cathie! There's a wee lass wants to say hello," Mr McKenzie called out before leading the way to the back room where his wife was sitting in a big armchair, knitting.

"Hello, Rosie. It's good of you to call in. I see Jim has chosen a nice bunch for you today."

It took Rosie a moment to realise Jim was Mr McKenzie.

"I helped to choose, too."

"Aye, she did that and it's a good eye for colours she has," Mr McKenzie said, making Rosie feel all warm inside again.

"And what's that? Don't tell me. Did Neil give you the other wee bunch? He's a good lad and enjoys seeing you when he's here."

"Nan!" Neil's face was even redder when Rosie grinned at him.

"Well, you'd better go if your mam is waiting for the flowers. Maybe Neil could help you carry them across the street." Mrs McKenzie winked at her grandson. "Come and say hello the next time, Rosie."

"Aye, let's go," Neil said.

They didn't talk, but it was nice walking beside the bigger boy and he didn't seem to mind carrying the flowers.

"Thanks," Rosie said, as she took the flowers. "And thanks for the wee posy. It's lovely."

"See you next time." And Neil was off, running back across the road.

When Rosie went indoors, Mam came out of the kitchen.

"Oh, there you are. I was beginning to think you'd got lost in amongst the flowers. Thanks, love, they look bonnie."

Taking the big bunch, Mam laid them carefully on the table.

"Run away and get your hands washed so we can get going."

Rosie had managed to hide the posy behind her back till she reached her room. She was lucky to have a room to herself, but if another bairn arrived, she'd have to share.

She sniffed in the scent of the herbs and roses, wishing they could last for ever. Maybe one day she'd have her own garden.

* * * *

"Well, Mrs McKenzie, I hope you're as proud of that painting as I am of you."

Rosie swung round to accept her husband's hug.

"Thanks, Neil. But you're the gardener who produces the magic."

"We both do. It's one of your best."

They watched other people enjoy the results of their work.

She never failed to count her blessings that she and Neil had kept in touch. Once he'd finished agricultural college and she had developed her talent at art school, they'd started their own enchanted garden.

She turned to him now.

"There's something even more wonderful to look forward to next spring." Rosie patted her tummy and watched the delight spread across her husband's face. "Our own special, magical creation." ■

Illustration by Kirk Houston.

The Icing On
The Cake

by Patsy Collins

W HEN Lydia first returned to the town where she'd grown up, nothing was as she remembered. The field where she played was now a housing estate. The library only opened part-time and her old school had become a wine bar. OK, so that last one seemed a definite improvement.

Actually, a lot of the changes were for the better. Lydia was no longer a spotty kid with braces, but a successful career woman. The high street had smartened up and the once rather uninspiring Tuesday market now included farmers' produce and an artisan baker.

The traditional August Bank Holiday fete had also gone up in the world. The flower tent was a proper marquee instead of a tent borrowed from the Scouts. And they now had a "Bake Off" style event.

Lydia was told about that by a colleague when she'd spent a couple of days in her new office in preparation for the permanent move.

"That sounds fun," Lydia said. "I haven't done much lately, but back when I lived round here I was quite good at cake making."

"Have a go, then. Apparently the same woman always wins. It'd be good to have a change."

Lydia winning a cooking contest would be a change, all right. As she'd said, she was good at school, but Gemima had beaten her every time. Only just, but she always won.

It wasn't so much that she never won which annoyed Lydia. She had a few trophies for sporting events and was always top of the class in anything mathematical, so coming second in one subject didn't really bother her.

Or rather, it wouldn't have if anyone other than Gemima had beaten her. The girl was just so irritating!

∗   ∗   ∗   ∗

Lydia was given a few days off to sort out her move, but she'd gone in to work as soon as she had internet.

The wait at reception for her new security pass shouldn't have taken long as there was just one person ahead of her. The young woman asked about the administration support vacancy, but couldn't seem to make up her mind if she actually wanted to apply.

"Don't know if I'm quite suitable . . . I expect lots of other people will be interested."

That was no way to make a good impression! Lydia felt herself getting irritated even before she realised it was Gemima. Obviously she was one of the things which hadn't changed.

Lydia reached across, picked up a form and gave it to her.

"It says which qualifications and what experience are needed. If you have them, fill it in and send it back." Lydia gave a tight smile and a look she hoped would encourage Gemima to stop dithering and leave.

"It's Lydia, isn't it? We went to school together . . ."

Lydia wanted to say she was busy, but somehow ended up agreeing to meet Gemima for coffee. They had cake with it and this led to a conversation about the forthcoming baking competition.

"I'm going to have a try," Lydia said. "I've heard the same person always wins. Are you going to enter?"

"I think so." Gemima didn't sound at all sure.

Lydia wanted to shake her — a feeling she remembered well.

That evening, Lydia looked up the cake competition online and discovered two things.

Firstly, that this year it was to be a butterfly version of a Bakewell tart — "two classics turned into one delicious work of art". Secondly, Gemima was the woman who always won. Lydia formed a plan . . .

For starters, she arranged that the job interviews for the position Gemima had eventually applied for would be on the same day as the cake competition. Not at the same time – she wasn't totally heartless.

"Odd time to have them," the boss said. "In the evening on a Bank Holiday."

"Yes, it will demonstrate candidates' flexibility."

Lydia practised for ages with her butterfly cakes. She used a frangipani mix to replicate the filling of a Bakewell tart.

The ground almonds not only produced a rich, satisfying texture, but they also stopped the mixture rising into peaks. Perfectly level tops allowed Lydia to create a mini version of the traditional white icing and chocolate feather pattern on each individual cake.

When cut really carefully, they made lovely, intricate butterfly wings.

She added amaretto liqueur to the icing to give extra flavour and a sophisticated touch. Underneath she used a generous amount of jam.

Not the traditional raspberry used in Bakewells, but tangy cherry conserve. That set off the luscious almond flavour perfectly.

On the day of the competition everything was going well. Her sponge batter didn't curdle. She didn't spill any on to the paper cases, where it would have scorched and spoiled the overall look.

The cakes cooked evenly and came out perfectly level.

Then she spotted the judges coming round with microphones to talk to contestants as they worked. They reached her just as she was adding the chocolate icing stripes to the pristine white icing, ready to create the feather pattern.

Lydia chatted to the judges and smiled confidently as she worked. It took a little longer than it should have done, perhaps, but the judges finally went on to Gemima, who was already assembling her cakes.

"Very important to jam the filling right in," Gemima said in an overly loud and high-pitched voice.

What? Quite the opposite was true. It had to be done very gently or bakers risked pushing the cake out of shape or getting crumbs in the smooth filling. Lydia looked across. Gemima was doing it gently – almost tentatively, actually, which was typical of her!

Lydia quickly piped in creamy filling and placed the wings in position.

"I must be careful not to jam the wings on too tightly," she heard Gemima say.

Lydia's eye fell on her still-full pot of cherry conserve. Gemima had tried to warn her! It was now too late to pull off the wings, scrape out the filling and start again.

Lydia slid the pot out of sight. She'd rely on the tastiness of her filling with its alcoholic extra ingredient and pretend the thought of doing anything with jam had never entered her head.

"Time's up, everyone. Step away from the cakes."

Most entries were fairly good, but Gemima's were incredible. She'd toasted flaked almonds to a soft biscuit colour. Others she'd iced individually in various subtle colours.

The cake wings were iced, too, and then each flake of almond carefully placed to form an image of butterfly wings. They were exquisite.

The judges walked round and were complimentary about all the entries, even those which were frankly rather ordinary. It was clear, however, that only two were in contention for the top prize.

Much was made of the clever way Lydia had adapted the traditional look. Would that trump Gemima's innovative take on the theme?

Then the taste test.

"Is that amaretto? Wonderful flavour," one judge said.

"The sponge is lovely and the icing beautiful. But it's traditional to have jam in Bakewell tarts," another remarked. "If you'd included a sharpish-flavoured one that would have set off the rest to perfection."

Gemima won, of course. She was presented with a trophy, showered with praise, asked to pose for pictures and then she had to go.

Both of them did, in fact. They almost crashed into each other as they rushed out of the building.

"Not staying for the raffle?" Lydia asked.

"Can't. I've got a job interview. I took your advice and applied." Gemima glanced at her watch.

"I'll give you a lift," Lydia said. In the car she interrogated Gemima on her academic record and familiarity with the relevant procedures. Surprisingly, Gemima was able to reply promptly that she did indeed have the qualifications and experience needed.

Lydia changed tack.

"They need someone who can follow written instructions, work under pressure, capable of working independently but also a team player . . ."

"Well, I do try . . . The baking competition is tense, but I follow the recipe and I . . ." She blushed.

"But you don't lose your nerve and forget to put the jam in?"

"I'm so sorry . . . Anyone could make a mistake like that, especially as it was your first time." Her blush deepened. "I did try to give you a hint, but didn't want to actually say and draw attention to it."

Lydia believed her. Gemima did have the qualities she'd mentioned, and she got results and had a great deal of integrity.

Gemima had always been a good person, just as she'd always been irritating due to her complete lack of confidence, despite her skills and intelligence.

Lydia was right about Gemima's nerves, though, and had known she'd go to pieces before the interview panel. The competition took her mind off it and winning gave her the confidence to sell her good points.

Lydia drove right round the roundabout.

"Let's drop off my car and have a drink."

"But the job interview?"

"Oh, yes, thanks for reminding me." She pulled over into the next lay-by and made a call. "Hi. Lydia here . . . Yes, fine thanks. I've interviewed Miss Gemima May and she seems an ideal candidate. I recommend she be appointed. OK, thank you. See you tomorrow."

She turned to an open-mouthed Gemima and grinned.

"Congratulations. Again." ■

Oban, Argyll And Bute

The impressive McCaig's Tower dominates views of Oban, the west-coast fishing town that is also a popular tourist resort.

The structure was built by a local banker named McCaig between 1895 and 1902. Outwardly, it resembles the Colosseum. Take the short uphill walk from the centre of the town, though, and you won't find an amphitheatre, but a grassy hilltop surrounded by the tower walls and magnificent views of the town.

Looking seawards, the island of Kerrera is located within the bay. Day trips to the nearest islands of Mull, Iona and Staffa are popular with tourists. Oban is also the port for the Caledonian MacBrayne ferry sailings to Barra and South Uist in the Western Isles.

Visitors who elect to stay on the mainland will find plenty to see and do. The "Seafood Capital of Scotland" offers beautiful beaches, castles, gardens, museums and lots of independent shops.

And why not discover the fascinating history of one of the smallest whisky distilleries in Scotland? Built in 1794, it became the focus for the development of the town, and produces a fine single malt.

Second Time Around

by Eirin Thompson

PATRICE was up to her eyes. Someone had just brought in nearly twenty cardboard boxes of potential new stock. Fortunately, no actual customers had arrived yet and, as it had been raining, none might come for a while.

"I didn't realise when I took the job that I'd be so busy," she'd told her sister, Phoebe. "I imagined myself sitting behind the counter, reading the pick of the books that people donated, being nice to the customers and putting the money in the till."

"Are you regretting taking it on?" Phoebe enquired.

"No! Not at all. It's good for me to have something meaningful to do."

This was true. When Patrice had retired, she'd wondered if she might have to move to avoid being too isolated. She loved the little gate-lodge where she'd lived since her thirties, but it was pretty well in the wilds.

The "big house" to which it was attached – Drillcourt Manor – was a kind of living museum, which attracted visitors, particularly at the weekends. But there was no local shop, or pub, or other social hub.

It had occurred to Patrice that a move to town might be necessary, if she wasn't to become a recluse.

Then a friend told her that Drillcourt Manor was opening a second-hand bookshop in the courtyard, as a fund-raiser to help with the never-ending maintenance bills, and volunteers were being sought to run it.

"It will only be open Fridays, Saturdays and Sundays, at least to begin

with," Mrs Mountford, who ran the manor, had told her.

"We need one person to manage it and a few more bodies to help out and to cover the manager's leave. I'm afraid the whole thing would have to be done on a voluntary basis, if we're to make any money from it."

Patrice had gone home and thought. The courtyard was just a stroll from the gate-lodge, and the commitment was only three days a week.

She had put in an application, attended an interview and, to her surprise, been offered the manager's role.

The courtyard premises were fitted out with shelving, and an appeal went out to the group known as the "Friends of Drillcourt" for initial book donations, with the plan to open the doors at the start of the following month.

Mrs Mountford asked Patrice for her clothing size, as the shop staff were to wear matching fisherman's-style smocks as their casual uniform.

And now here she was, six weeks in, and the shop was thriving. This morning's twenty boxes were exceptional, but Patrice and her team had taken in a steady stream of donations since opening, and there had been no shortage of customers.

"It's having a great knock-on effect on the coffee shop," Mrs Mountford revealed. "In fact, if things continue this way, they're going to need more staff.

"Not everyone wants to see round the manor, especially if they've done that once or twice before, but the combination of books, coffee and our lovely grounds seems to be an attractive package for many."

This morning, Patrice was on her own. She did her best to lift and drag the cardboard boxes away from the walkways, but really she needed to go through them as soon as possible and distribute the contents around the appropriate displays.

At the tinkling sound of the little bell over the door, Patrice turned round.

It was Neil, one of the volunteer gardeners, who'd popped into the bookshop a few times. Today, he was bearing a tray.

"One pot of Earl Grey," he said. "The girls in the coffee shop told me that's your usual order."

"How kind!" Patrice exclaimed.

"Looks like someone's been having quite a clear-out," Neil observed, nodding at the sea of boxes.

"Yes – it's a family who're moving to New Zealand. There seems to be everything from children's picture books and teen fiction to crime novels and the classics – a real treasure trove."

"I can't imagine giving away my entire collection of books – they're the story of my life," Neil commented. "But I suppose you can't take a whole library to the other side of the world."

"My little house doesn't really give me much room for clutter," Patrice told him. "But I make an exception for my books."

"Would you like some help to unpack this lot?" Neil offered. "The grass-cutting contractors have just arrived, and I don't much like being out in the gardens when they're zooming about."

"Are you sure?" Patrice asked.

"I know the shop lay-out by now," Neil replied, "and, of course, it gives me a great opportunity to see what's come in before anyone else does."

∗   ∗   ∗   ∗

Elaine, another bookshop volunteer, was holding the fort while Patrice ate her lunch at a picnic table. The afternoon was still, with scarcely a breeze to disturb the baking heat.

Further down the newly cut grass, a young family were playing football and picnickers were spread out on rugs.

"Mind if I join you?" It was Neil again, carrying a bottle of water and something in a wrapper.

"Please – be my guest," Patrice replied.

Neil unfolded a sandwich – they had both wrapped up their food in reusable beeswax sheets.

"I'm not exactly an eco-warrior, but I try to do my bit," he said.

"I suppose, working in a second-hand bookshop, which is, after all, a form of recycling, I can now boast that I'm employed in the environmentally friendly sector," Patrice answered with a smile.

"What did you do before? If you don't mind me asking."

"I was a translator – you know, foreign languages. I was part of a small collective and we hired an office together in town. How about you?"

"I lectured at the agricultural college for most of my career, but when a generous redundancy package came along, I jumped.

"I needed something to do, though, so I worked as a taxi driver for a few years. I enjoyed driving, but more and more I was attracted to spending time outdoors with nature, and now I couldn't be happier."

"My garden's tiny, but it seems to be facing in the right direction, because it's sunny all the time in summer."

"I hear you live in the gate-lodge just down the lane."

"That's me. I certainly can't complain about the commute to work. Do you come far?"

"I drive out from town – this end, though. It takes about twenty-five minutes."

Patrice checked her watch.

"My time's up. I must get back to the shop."

Neil rose to his feet as Patrice stood, and she was struck by the old-fashioned chivalry of the gesture. For the first time, it occurred to her that Neil's interest in her might be something more than merely friendly.

Up until now, she'd felt completely relaxed around him – he was simply a colleague, or perhaps even a kindred spirit, of around the same age.

Suddenly, she was supremely conscious that he was a man and she was a woman, and a warm blush crept into her cheeks.

"Elaine will be wondering where I've got to," she mumbled, and lifting her beeswax wrapper and empty teacup, she hurried off.

$$*\quad*\quad*\quad*$$

"Patrice? Patrice?"

It was Elaine, snapping her back to consciousness; she'd been miles away – or years away, to be more accurate.

"I was just saying, with all this up-to-date crime fiction, we could perhaps mount a special display – what do you think?"

"Yes. Yes, of course. That's a great idea."

"Is something up, Patrice? Are you feeling OK? You don't seem yourself."

"No, I'm fine. Just a bit distracted. Do you ever get that? You know, where you can't seem to concentrate on the matter in hand?"

"All the time – story of my life. It used to get me into trouble at school."

The mention of school touched a nerve – for that was where Patrice's current distraction had begun.

She and Todd had started going out in the sixth form. They were both prefects – sensible, diligent, destined for a successful future, it seemed.

They'd gone to different universities, but not far apart, and their romance persisted.

After graduation, they'd got engaged.

Patrice had found a job with a translation agency and Todd wasn't far behind, starting as a junior in an architect's office.

They weren't in any rush to marry, but they were in no doubt that this was what they both wanted.

Phoebe would be Patrice's bridesmaid and Todd's brother, Colin, would be his best man. They thought perhaps the Greek islands for the honeymoon.

And then, one evening, the police arrived at Patrice's parents' house and asked to speak to her. She was so young and inexperienced that she had no idea what they could possibly want.

When they said Todd had been killed in a road accident, she was absolutely convinced they had made a mistake. But they hadn't.

Patrice had been twenty-five years old when she lost Todd. She'd never looked at another man since.

"There. I've actually managed to make a whole display of female crime writers on one table," Elaine announced. "What do you think?"

"Excellent," Patrice replied, giving herself a mental shake. "We women must be a darker lot than we're sometimes credited with."

* * * *

Patrice sat in her garden that evening after work. She had a glass of wine on the patio table in front of her and a paperback novel in her lap, but she paid little attention to either. She was thinking about Neil.

It wasn't at all certain that he liked her in anything other than a platonic way. He might be happy as he was – retired from the demands of a career, pottering about the Drillcourt grounds.

But if he wasn't entirely satisfied with his life, if he wanted something more – companionship, even romance . . .?

Patrice had seldom asked herself over the years if she was perhaps missing something by not having a relationship.

She had simply kept on keeping on – going to work, looking after the gate-lodge, reading, seeing friends, enjoying Phoebe's children, even doing a bit of cross-stitch when boredom threatened.

She had rather assumed that this was how her life would continue for ever, and she was at a loss to explain how now, at the age of sixty, she was unable to concentrate on a rave-reviewed novel because she couldn't stop thinking about a man.

Patrice imagined sitting here, by the fruit trees, sharing her bottle of wine with Neil and talking about books.

"Because of Todd, I'll always have been someone else's to begin with," she mused. "But that doesn't mean I can't bring love and joy to someone else."

As for making a life change – some people even upped and left and went on new adventures in another hemisphere!

Patrice collected up her glass and novel and went inside.

Tomorrow morning, she'd locate Neil in the grounds and bring him his Americano and something sweet from the coffee shop.

Perhaps all he wanted was to be friends, and that would be just fine. But if they could mean more to each other, then Patrice reckoned she was ready to try that, too.

It had taken her a long time to get here, but now she deserved a second chance at love. ■

Abbotsford

This is one stately residence that's worth writing home about. Once the home of Sir Walter Scott, the iconic Baronial-style dwelling sits on the south side of the River Tweed in the Scottish Borders.

The Scottish historical novelist purchased the modest dwelling before his writing prowess earned him the money to create a grand mansion from its very humble beginnings as Cartley Hole farm.

He extended it, adding a library, grand dining-room and even an armoury, the large collection of which includes the gun, dirk and sword of Rob Roy.

Here Scott entertained politicians, writers and noblemen. The Abbotsford that we see today is built on the author's literary success and, despite near-bankruptcy due to the 1825 UK-wide banking crisis, remains a legacy of the great things he achieved.

Set in acres of beautiful grounds, the formal Regency gardens were tended by the highly respected gardener William Bogie.

Scott's epic poems and classic novels have stood the test of time.

Among the many great things he did was discover the "lost" Crown Jewels of Scotland, and he was rewarded with a baronetcy.

Sir Walter Scott died in the dining-room of Abbotsford at the age of sixty-one and is buried alongside his wife in Dryburgh Abbey.

A Little Bird

by Nicky Bothoms

O H, no!"

Leaning forward, Sarah spread the newspaper across the kitchen table, skim-reading the article underneath the bold headline.

It was as just she feared. Would her husband miss the newspaper if she just happened to slide it straight into the recycling bin?

"Sarah!" A well-timed whoop came from the living-room. "It's that time of year again!"

Drat. She'd forgotten about the digital copy sent to his tablet.

Sarah let loose a despairing groan. For the past five years, Robert had entered this photography competition, organised by a local club which usually invited professional photographers to act as judges.

Robert had tasted a drop of success three years ago when he had gained a Highly Commended. Ever since then, he had been trying to replicate – or better – his achievement, confiding that he hoped one day to be placed in the top three.

The problem was – well, Robert took it all just a little too seriously. Suddenly, every photo he took – and he took many beautiful photos throughout the year – had to be crazily creative.

The simple joy of his hobby was entirely lost in the lead-up to the competition. Nothing was ever good enough.

And it was that overly fussy approach which lost him the competition, at least in Sarah's opinion. Throughout their home, every wall was adorned with framed snapshots of their life, from the silly to the sublime, each one filled with laughter and love.

It was impossible to walk around the house and not be reminded of a memory from last month, last year, or even the last decade. When Robert didn't overthink things, his photos were delightful.

But would he be told? He would not.

"That's all amateur!" he would cry without looking up from the many professional photography magazines. She often bit her tongue against the observation that the competition was for amateurs. Talented amateurs, but amateurs, nonetheless. That was the whole point.

Now, taking a deep breath, Sarah folded up the newspaper and set it to one side, steeling herself against the inevitable.

"We'll be heading out, then?" she called, already reaching for her

jacket hanging by the back door. It was photography competition time. She would just have to endure, as she always did.

Of course, "endure" was a little strong. She did enjoy the outings into the local woodlands which Robert insisted they embark upon, ever determined to capture the most spectacular scenery from the beautiful surroundings of their village.

Every year, she rediscovered a hidden nook or overlooked cranny from which to admire the countryside, and always something new to marvel over.

They were very lucky to have several viewpoints dotted around the local woodlands, offering different panoramas across the valley and towards the distant hills.

She tried to suggest one as an option to Robert, remarking that the turn of season painted the trees a variety of pretty colours. But he was having none of it.

"Autumnal hues?" he harrumphed. "Too obvious!"

And on he stomped, ever questing for the perfect shot. Last year, she had amused herself with the observation – rather witty, she decided – that Robert would never see the wood for the trees.

With a last lingering look across the valley, Sarah followed Robert along the muddy path, worn down by countless other feet which had trekked this way.

He never got that far ahead anyway. He was always stopping to investigate a potential arty angle or creative composition.

While she was admiring her surroundings, a trill of birdsong rang out through the trees. Surprised by the proximity, Sarah stopped short and looked around, curious as to where the bird might be hiding.

She was swiftly proven wrong. The robin was not hiding at all. In fact, it was perched upon a thin silver birch branch, regarding her with its bright black eye, its head tilting first one way then the other while he – yes, she decided it was a he – made up his mind about her.

Funny, she had always associated robins with winter. Maybe it was all those Christmas cards which depicted the snowy scene and a boldly positioned robin.

Suddenly, with an elegant swoop from branch to ground, he flitted into the undergrowth, chirping his annoyance about this oversized intruder in his territory.

Her laughter slipped out before she could stop it. Hastily, Sarah clapped her hand over her mouth, wondering if anyone would think she was mad for laughing by herself in the woods.

"Sarah?" Robert called from a short way ahead. "Is everything all right?"

She hurried to catch up with him.

"Yes, I was just laughing at a robin."

"A robin?" he echoed before shaking his head. He hoisted the strap of his camera more firmly over his shoulder. "I'll never win the competition with a photo of something so ordinary. Come on, let's try up this way."

Sarah wasn't sure she agreed.

While Robert huffed and puffed his way through the undergrowth, abandoning the path for his art, she hesitated, hoping to catch another glimpse of the little bird.

Her patience was soon rewarded. The robin – she was quite sure it was the same one – emerged from the safety of a bush, chasing another small bird away with angry chittering.

He came to a halt on a branch, his red chest puffed out. Quickly, Sarah pulled her phone from her pocket and snapped a picture, allowing the camera with all the fancy automatic features to arrange the composition.

"You're very photogenic," she informed the little bird.

He hopped to and fro on the branch, seemingly pleased by the compliment, before spreading his wings and disappearing into the nearby bush again.

She hadn't even known that robins were commonly found in woodlands. Yet he certainly seemed comfortable in his surroundings.

She turned and followed Robert, a little alarmed that she might lose him if he continued his adventure beyond the path much further.

Fortunately, he had come to a halt in a clearing and was fussing over this and that, muttering beneath his breath all the while.

Initially, Sarah idled away the time by finding somewhere to sit – she was quite the dab hand at finding a comfy stump or rock – but she was distracted by what she thought was a familiar song from somewhere high above.

She stopped and craned her neck, trying to catch another glimpse of the robin. Not that she was an expert on the call of a robin, by any means. She was going to feel very silly indeed if an entirely different bird suddenly swooped down from the branches.

"What is it?" Robert glanced up from fiddling around with a portable tripod he kept in his bag of equipment.

"I thought I heard the robin again, but . . ." She was interrupted by an almost indignant chirp.

On a small branch, on the other side of the clearing, sat the robin. Acting as though he had been sitting there the whole time! He was definitely a little character.

"There he is!"

Robert blinked.

"How do you know it's the same robin?"

Sarah laughed.

"I don't. But it seems like him. I think we're in his territory." She took out her smartphone and typed in the species of bird, bringing up pages upon pages of information.

"Look," she said, tapping on a page and holding it out for Robert to squint at. "They have quite large territories for their size."

Robert grunted, his attention already reverting to his own preoccupation. The robin, too, had lost his curiosity in them, spying something far more interesting on the forest floor and hopping down towards it.

But Sarah had an idea.

"I took a photo," she said, swiftly changing the screen on her smartphone from the internet browser to the photo album instead. She held out the phone so that Robert could see the image on the screen. "The phone did all the work."

Intrigued, he forgot about his tripod and leaned forward so that he could better see.

"That's a great photo," he enthused, focus on the competition easing for a moment.

Nimbly, Sarah spun around on her ball of her foot and held the phone high above her, catching them both in the frame of the screen.

"Another great one." She laughed, noting her beaming smile and Robert's surprised half-grin.

"I'm sure it is." He smiled, beginning to turn back to his tripod.

"Oh, come on, Robert," she implored. "Let's have some fun."

He hesitated, glancing between Sarah and his tripod, seemingly torn. Then, with a little self-conscious laugh, he unscrewed the camera from its perch and looped the strap around his neck.

"All right," he agreed, beginning to grin. "What first?"

"Anything which catches our eye!" She beamed, throwing her arms out to indicate the splendour of their surroundings. "Look, what about that tree? It looks like it's trying to reach out and grab us from this angle."

"Go on, then."

Spurred on by his eagerness, Sarah quickly adopted a fearful pose, pretending to evade the outstretched branches of the tree. Robert clicked away with his camera.

Next, it was her turn. She used her phone to snap an image of Robert playing daredevil, balancing on a branch which grew over a steep drop. It was just a clever trick of angles, though. Robert had helped her to line up the shot.

Soon, laughter filled the small clearing as the pair of them indulged in increasingly silly poses, creating an entire imaginary adventure from their woodland surroundings.

It was only when Sarah's phone alerted her to a low battery that they decided it was time to head back home.

With a practised hand, Robert tidied up the forgotten tripod and they trudged back through the undergrowth towards the path, keeping in companionable step with one another.

Just as they emerged from the line of trees, Robert drew to a halt.

"Would you look at this?" He chuckled, flicking through the photos on the screen of his digital camera.

Sarah peered over his shoulder.

"Oh, but they're brilliant!" She giggled. She had brought the fun and Robert had brought the skill.

"Yes, they are, but look more closely."

Frowning, Sarah peered a little harder, searching each photo with more attention. In the corner of the first was . . . And then near the bottom of the second . . . And in the top of the third . . .

"It's the robin!"

"It is." Robert was laughing outright now. "Every single shot." He was quiet for a moment. "Which one do you think is . . ." he paused, searching for the right word ". . . the most fun?"

"Fun?" she echoed in disbelief. "But the competition . . ."

He shrugged, looking a little embarrassed.

"I haven't had much fun with it these last few years. Maybe it's time to change that."

"I think that's a perfect idea!" Sarah declared. Excitedly, she clicked through to one of the final images they had taken.

They were both flushed with running around and their expressions bright with laughter, and the little robin was perched perfectly in the centre of the frame, just above their touching heads.

"This one. All three of us!"

"Perfect." Robert took the camera back and kissed the tip of her nose. "But if I win, I'm not sharing credit with him."

"When you win," Sarah corrected with a grin.

She had a feeling that the annual photography competition might just be a little different this year. Maybe it was something a little bird had told her! ■

Illustration by Shutterstock.

The Wild Geese

by Shona Partridge

THE girl stood leaning on the Embankment, looking down at the Thames. The river flowed on for ever, taking time along with it. Two years had flowed past this spot since she had run away to London.

Running away seemed rather a melodramatic phrase for what she had done, Margaret Ogilvy thought. But still, she had been running away. Running away from a broken heart.

In the first few months, Margaret had found she'd taken the broken heart along with her when she'd fled. Yet she had also found it was true, that time did help.

Yes, she had been lonely, but books had been her salvation. She had haunted the library on her days off and music had helped, too. Every month she bought the cheapest concert ticket available and lost herself in Mozart or Beethoven.

Now she was wondering what to do with the rest of her afternoon off. It was a cold day in early November and she really should find a warm tearoom.

The gusts of wind were getting stronger and colder as she stood there, reminiscing. Yet the river held her almost hypnotised by its hurrying currents. In a strange way, it reminded Margaret of her own river back home.

It was the gulls, she realised, and the salt smell of the sea, blown upriver on the east wind. It smelled so like her own north-east lands. And these gulls looked just the same to her as the ones that followed the plough on the farm at home.

At first she'd thought it was her imagination. A faint honking of geese reached her ears, cutting into her consciousness through the roar and hubbub of London.

The honking grew louder and then she saw them overhead, a ragged skein of geese, silhouetted against the low winter sun.

Margaret almost forgot she was in London, as she felt pulled back to her own heartlands. She was struck by a wave of homesickness so strong it nearly stopped her breath.

Now she recalled all the other birds of the farmlands. The jaunty lapwings and the curlews with their plaintive cry. The cloud-dipping skylarks and even the silent, swooping barn owls.

But it was the geese that were crying to her to come home. The noisy winter geese, suddenly appearing overhead and showing the way north, as sure as an arrow might.

There was a power pulling her back, stronger even than the love she thought she held for Alasdair. Stronger even than her own pride, and her pride was a powerful thing.

It had driven her here, to a city of strangers.

Yet I won't regret it, she thought. No, not any of it. She had grown in strength and understanding these past two years.

And more than anything she needed to see her family again. Margaret thought of the two years of birthdays and Christmases she had missed. And for what? What she now regarded as a foolish infatuation.

The world looked very different at nearly twenty-one than it had at eighteen, she thought.

The skein of wild geese reminded Margaret she had missed another harvest. Well, I won't miss another Christmas with my family, she decided. I want to go home. I need to go home as much as the wild geese flying back to the straths. I've stayed away long enough.

* * * *

The long train journey north gave her plenty of time to think. Memories flooded back so vividly. And somehow, on that journey,

Margaret Ogilvy became the Meg of girlhood once again.

Alasdair Ross had been the love of her young life. He had joined in childhood adventures with Meg and her brothers.

They played at being explorers, at cowboys and Indians; they ran races and had archery competitions. Meg ran nearly as fast as the boys and was often twice as fearless, fording the river to fetch the ball that had gone right out of the field and not being afraid to walk past the haunted shieling, even in the dark.

Meg's father was one of Lord Ross's tenants and her family had been on this land for generations.

Then Alasdair had gone away to boarding school and the childhood friendship was severed. She rarely saw him after that, and even when she did, there was a new formality in their exchanges.

And so it was until Meg turned eighteen. Alasdair was home from the university and had come along to watch the harvest and then stayed to help, stooking the barley with Meg and her brothers.

And when the sudden rainstorm caught them all, he'd sheltered her under his jacket and come back to their house to dry off, staying for his tea.

That day had marked a new beginning for their friendship.

The harvest was in and safe for another year. On Sunday they would all troop to church for the service of Thanksgiving, but this Friday night was given over to music and dancing.

The village hall was strung with paper lanterns and on the stage the fiddlers were tuning up. There was a new awareness between them when Alasdair took her in his arms for a waltz.

Soon they were walking out together and it was not long before Meg realised that she loved Alasdair. One day, not long before he had to go back to university, he told her of his plans.

"Rob will inherit, of course, being the eldest, so I can choose the life I want." He hoisted himself up on to the old boundary wall that had marked her family's land for generations.

"My law degree will always give me a lucrative career. How would you feel about settling in Edinburgh? What if I said I might want to marry you one day, Meg?"

Meg wasn't sure what Alasdair expected her to say. The direct gaze of his blue eyes seemed to challenge her.

"Oh, Alasdair, time enough to settle down when you have finished your degree." Meg was not letting on that she hoped he was being serious.

"Besides, I want to do my teacher training." She didn't want him to think he was the centre of her universe, even if that was how she really felt.

"Well," he said, "what if we became unofficially engaged until I graduate?"

So that was how Meg had found herself to be Alasdair's fiancée.

"But let's not tell anyone yet, I don't want all that fuss," he said.

So there had been no ring and no announcement. He'd gone back to

It's A Dog's Life

While one dog's pulling me this way,
The other one's pulling me that.
It's at moments like these
When I can neither please
That I wish I was owned by a cat.

But as soon as we reach the field's
    entrance
And I let them both off for a run,
It's at moments like these
That life is a breeze
As they rush around under the sun.

Back home we're tired and we're
    drowsy,
So we all share the sofa to rest.
It's at moments like these,
When relaxed and at ease
That I feel my life's doubly blessed.

John Darley

university and all Meg had were occasional letters. Still, he'd be busy with his studies, she told herself, making excuses for him.

But then his brother Rob had died in an accident and Alasdair became the heir to the lands of Howe.

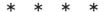

Meg broke her journey in Edinburgh to visit her mother's sister. Auntie Jean had been a teacher before she married and had always encouraged Meg in her studies.

"I'm told you were the cleverest girl in the school, and there's no reason why you shouldn't go on and do your teacher training," her aunt had said two summers ago when Meg had left the school.

Auntie Jean raised the subject again while they strolled in the late autumn sun in Princes Street Gardens.

"The boys will take on the farm in time and they will find wives. You'll be wanting your own place, Meg.

"Of course you will. Too many women in a farm kitchen makes for bad bannocks."

Meg laughed.

"Of course you're right," Meg agreed.

She knew her love of books and learning would never leave her. Meg wanted to share her love of knowledge and she might have a chance to do that yet.

She had choices to make and plans to form.

Yes, she loved the land, but she loved learning even more. She felt a new resolve to take up her studies again. Ideally, she would get a job at the local school once she completed her training.

Meg knew it was time to revisit the old ambitions she had put on hold because of Alasdair.

No man was going to define who she was or what she did with the rest of her life.

Back on the train north, Meg allowed herself to relive the truth of why she'd run away to London. The sharp edges of her memories were softened now, but still vivid with remembered emotion.

She recalled the day Alasdair had brought her flowers and then he'd broken her heart.

"You must see we can't marry now," he said. "Not now I've inherited the title and the estate."

The vase of flowers slipped from her hands, shattering on the kitchen flagstones. Her heart felt like the shards of glass littering the hard stone floor.

For the laird's second son to marry the daughter of his largest tenant farmer might seem reasonable. For the heir to the lands of Howe to do so was simply not acceptable. Land married land, and that was the way it had always been.

"I'm sorry, Meg. I didn't mean to hurt you and I wanted to tell you myself that I will be marrying Lord Strathallan's daughter next summer. We're announcing it at the harvest dance on Friday and I didn't want it to come as a shock to you."

How on earth could he be so unfeeling? Of course she was shocked. Meg felt betrayed and humiliated. Even though they had not been officially engaged, the whole strath knew they were walking out together.

How could she stay here and stand to be gossiped about, or worse, pitied? No, it would not do at all.

Very quickly Meg had formed her plan to get a job as far away as possible. Besides, she had always wanted to see London.

It was fairly easy for her to find work as a maid at a big house in Kensington as so many girls had left service after the war.

The work was hard and the hours were long, but there was no-one from home to remind her of Alasdair and what might have been.

The position had given Meg a guaranteed roof over her head. A settled place to live was the most important thing to her. And now, at last, that settled place would be her own home once again.

Perhaps it was not that Alasdair had been deliberately cold-hearted. It was just the way of the world, and by now she had made her peace with it.

After two years away, Meg realised she would not even dread meeting Alasdair in church or in the village one day. The river had moved on, past the place of hurting.

✶   ✶   ✶   ✶

Meg left her luggage at the station and walked home over fields crisping with frost. A low wind sang through the pine woods on the ridge behind the house.

She could see the kitchen window of the farmhouse and the shadow of her mother in front of the yellow light from the lamp. But she was not ready to go in quite yet. There was something she felt compelled to do first.

It was beyond logic, but Meg knew the geese must be acknowledged and thanked. She walked the short distance to the loch of Howe.

It had been a place of pilgrimage back into the mists of time and there had once been a crannog near its shores. Perhaps her own distant ancestors had watched the ancestors of these same geese. It did not seem far-fetched to Meg, but very likely.

Meg had known the geese would be there before her. They had led her here, after all. She gave silent thanks for her return.

A great crowd of geese was on the loch and, as she watched, more and more flew in to join them.

Their excited gabbling sounded for all the world like they were exchanging news and gossip, tales of their long travels over land and sea.

A journey like her own, focused on reaching just this one place on all the earth. Home. ■

Shutterstock.

Polesden Lacey, Surrey

Located less than five miles from Dorking, this eye-catching stately home has wonderful views over the rolling hills.

The first house to be constructed on the site dates back to the 14th century, but the core of the house we see today was built in 1822 by Thomas Cubitt, who was also responsible for developing grand London squares Belgravia and Bloomsbury.

Polesden Lacey was extensively refurbished in 1906 and society hostess and philanthropist Margaret Greville turned it into an Edwardian showpiece.

It houses many fine paintings, Maiolica, Meissen and Chinese ceramics and fine French furniture, with Margaret adding to the collection that her father – the MP and brewing magnate William McEwan – began.

Here, the widowed society hostess opened her doors to the social elite of the day, including politicians, celebrities and royals.

It's not hard to see why George VI and Elizabeth Bowes-Lyon chose to spend part of their honeymoon on this country estate following their wedding in 1923.

The house itself is set in 1,400 acres where you'll find ancient woodland (a Site of Special Scientific Interest), a walled rose garden and the only Graham Stuart Thomas designed Winter Garden left in existence.

The grounds are a magnet for some rare species, too, from bats to buzzards. Margaret Greville bequeathed the house to the National Trust in 1942.

Papa's Pasta Sauce

by Francesca Capaldi

I T had been a long day at work for Gina. As she parked her car on the drive she noticed the sun, low on the horizon, highlighting the red and yellow leaves on the trees. A Neapolitan song, frequently played on the family record player when she was a child, came to mind: "Malinconico Autunno". Sad Autumn.

Pushing the front door closed with her foot, she stretched and yawned. Opening her eyes, she noticed the date on the day-to-a-page calendar sitting on the hall table. As if she needed reminding.

No, she wouldn't think about that, not now.

"Hi, Lili, hi, Dan," she called up to her teenage children. There was a vague response from each of their bedrooms.

As she sloped off to the kitchen she was followed by Candy, the golden retriever. Gina patted her head.

"Suppose you want your dinner, too. I'll sort you out in a moment."

She went to the fridge, realising immediately there wasn't a lot there. On Fridays, she normally stopped by the supermarket on her way home to do shopping for the weekend, but the meetings had gone on a long time this evening and she hadn't had the energy.

John wasn't due home for another twenty minutes. Perhaps he could pick up something on his way back.

Looking out of the window, she tutted at the fading light. She'd never liked this time of year, with its ever-shorter days. But this year she had even more reason to feel despondent.

She pulled her mobile out of her bag and pressed John's name.

"You home now?" he asked.

"Yeah. I was wondering if you could pick up a takeaway en route."

"Sounds like a good idea. You must be as tired as me. I'm leaving here in five. Pizza OK?"

Illustration by André Leonard.

"Great. And yes, I am tired. But also . . . the date – tomorrow. I feel kind of weird."

"The date?"

"October the thirteenth."

"Oh, of course. That's understandable."

As she disconnected the call, Gina happened to glance up at the top of the freezer. There was a pot there, filled with something reddy-orange.

She dragged herself over and reached up to fetch it down. It was what she had dreaded.

The last pot of tomato pasta sauce, made by her father.

And it had defrosted. It must have been out all day. But how? Her eyes welled with tears she tried to sniff back, but it was no good.

Within a few seconds exasperation took over and she marched back into the hall before taking the stairs two steps at a time.

At the top she stood in the middle of the landing.

"Liliana! Dante!"

Both poked their heads out of their bedrooms.

"Did one of you go into the freezer this morning?"

Liliana put her hand up.

"Yeah, me. Only to get my bottle of water out."

Gina's daughter had a habit of placing it there each night so the following day, at school, she could have iced water for at least the morning.

"Bet you left the door open again, Lili," Dante said. His sister had done this once before, accidently defrosting the freezer.

Gina ignored this.

"And did you move anything to reach it?'

"Only a packet of peas, I think. And maybe a couple of other bits. But I put them back."

"Apart from the pot of pasta sauce. It was on top of the freezer."

Liliana's hand went to her mouth.

"Oh, Mum, I'm so sorry."

"It was the very − last − one." Gina felt the tears forming once again through the vexation.

"I must have forgotten −" Liliana started, before they heard the front door open.

"Oh, Lils! Papa's pasta sauce was special," her brother said.

Liliana started to well up, too.

"I know. It was an accident."

John stood at the bottom of the stairs holding up a brown paper carrier bag.

"Pizza delivery," he called with a smile. Slowly he lowered the bag. "What's wrong?'

"Lili left Papa's last pot of pasta sauce out of the freezer," Dan called down.

"Thanks for that." Liliana folded her arms, her bottom lip sticking out.

John put the bag down and put his arm around Gina. He reached out for Liliana as her first tears fell.

"I don't know what else to say but sorry."

John hugged them.

"I presume the sauce has defrosted, so not a lot we can do now. Perhaps we could have it with the pizza?" His face lit up as if he'd had a brilliant idea.

Gina stepped backwards.

"You don't understand. He'll never make that sauce again. That was the last of the ones we rescued from the freezer in his flat. I wanted to save it for a very special occasion."

"I know, love. But for what occasion in particular? You never say."

"I don't know. I can't decide." Gina slumped. She'd never been able to make her mind up. It wasn't as if she could have left it in the freezer for ever.

Though maybe that had been at the back of her mind. To have a little piece of him there for all time.

"Well, for now we've got dinner waiting and we ought to have it before it gets cold."

Gina shook her head.

"I'm not hungry. I'm going to bed."

Her husband and son watched her until the bedroom door closed.

"Oh, dear. Just the three of us then," John said.

He headed downstairs but hadn't reached the bottom before he realised the bag wasn't where he'd left it. When he saw the trail of brown paper, cardboard box and pizza along the floor, he groaned.

"Candy!"

Dante was down two minutes later, by which time John had cleared up the mess.

"Lili says she's not hungry. I know Mum's upset, but it is only one pot of sauce. We've got other things to remember Papa by."

"I know, son, but it's the anniversary of Papa Joe's death tomorrow."

John recalled the phone call, almost a year before, to say a neighbour had found him with his head down on one of the tables in his restaurant, as if he were asleep.

It had been an awful few months after, arranging the funeral, clearing Joe's things up and selling the business. Gina still hadn't recovered from it all.

"Think it's called anniversary grief."

Dante leaned against the wall.

"A year already? I do miss him a lot. He had so much life in him. What can we do for Mum, though?"

"I don't know."

"I guess we'd better eat that pizza before it gets cold."

John sucked his lips in.

"Bad news, I'm afraid. Candy got there first."

The dog was curled up in the corner of the kitchen, head on her outstretched paws, looking guilty and remorseful.

"Oh, Candy," Dante remonstrated. "Don't suppose it would have been as good as Papa's pizza, anyway."

"Probably not. Beans on toast?"

"Yeah. I'll do the toast, you do the beans. But first, I'll see how your mum is and you check on Liliana."

John followed his son up the stairs, considering the problem. But he hadn't a clue what to do.

The next morning, a Saturday, Gina lay on her back in bed. She was staring up at the ceiling, watching the swirling reflections of the beaded mobile they had hanging in the window.

This day last year . . . She'd had a dream about Papa last night, something about her being a teenager in the restaurant. As she'd awoken, she almost fancied she could smell the wonderful aroma of garlic and tomato.

Weren't people supposed to feel better after a year had gone by? She felt no different from the way she had when they'd received that awful telephone call.

She squeezed her eyes shut against the physical ache of loss. After losing her mum at twenty, it just wasn't fair to lose her dad before she'd even reached her fortieth birthday. He'd only been sixty-nine. No age at all these days.

They'd been going to take him on holiday last month, back to his home village in Italy. He hadn't visited in forty years and had been so looking forward to it.

"Why do we never go there?" she'd asked him as a teen.

"Ah, you know." He'd lifted his hands, palms outwards, and shrugged. "All the family are here. And when do I have the time, what with the restaurant?"

It was true the business stole away many long hours. She thought he might retire at sixty-five, but he'd carried on. Gina reckoned throwing himself into work had been his way of coping with losing her mother.

When he'd died, she'd sold the business to her cousin Luca. She'd had no inclination to take it on herself but at least it kept it in the family.

There was a knock on the door, quickly followed by Dante's voice.

"Mum? Dad?"

"What is it?" Gina called.

"Lili's not in her room. I've checked round the house and garden. I can't find her anywhere."

John and Gina as one leapt from the bed. She checked the clock.

"Lili likes her lie-ins at the weekend. It's not even eight o'clock yet."

In her daughter's room they found her bed hadn't been slept in. It was as neat as it had been when Gina made it yesterday morning.

Gina headed off for a tour of the house. It was unlikely Dante had missed anything, but she wanted to check for herself. She was at the back door letting Candy out when her son and husband caught up with her.

"Her phone's ringing but there's no reply," Dante said.

She shut the patio door.

"I'll ring the police.

John shook his head.

"No point. She's only been gone hours at most. And she's sixteen."

Gina slumped on to a dining chair, shivering in her nightie.

"What are we going to do?"

"Let's start by getting dressed."

By the time Gina got back downstairs, John had called on neighbours whose daughter was friends with Liliana. Dante had rung up a couple of friends whose sisters were mates with her. Neither had any success.

"Here, I've made you a cuppa." John handed her some tea.

"Thanks, you're a love." She clutched the cup with both hands, enjoying the warmth. "I wouldn't be so worried if it hadn't been for the business with the sauce. Oh, dear, I wish I hadn't got so upset."

"It's understandable. By the way, I put the sauce in the fridge."

"Thank you, but it doesn't seem quite so important now."

John stroked his chin.

"Perhaps we should try thinking like a teenage girl."

Gina pondered. What did she do, as a teenager, when she argued with her parents? There'd been some quarrels over working in the school holidays when she'd been an older teen, still at school.

She'd had a few strops over it, walking out a couple of times. Poor Mum and Papa. She'd never gone far though. Mostly over the road to the river, watching the water rush towards the sea.

She'd done much the same the first few months after Papa had died, standing opposite the restaurant, watching the tide get higher and lower. At times Liliana had joined her.

There was something calming about being by water. And being near the restaurant, though it belonged to Luca now, made her feel close to Papa.

"You OK, love? You seem miles away." John stroked her arm.

"I think I know where Lili might be."

She put the half-drunk tea down and fetched her keys from her bag.

"Where are we going?"

"You stay here in case she comes back. I won't be long."

The drive to the river took ten minutes. The low sun spread a golden wash of colour over the area.

Although it was warm for October, the beach and river areas were quieter today, not brimful of tourists as they often were in the summer.

Gina parked near the pier and walked along the riverside, past the ornamental pond, on to the road with its row of cafés. A small yacht passed by, causing ripples.

The swans, until now floating majestically on the water, bobbed up and down, yet seemed unfazed.

On the low wall overlooking the river, across the narrow road from the café, a girl in a tracksuit was sitting, her long, dark hair tied in a ponytail. Liliana.

She was swinging her legs as she looked out across the river, towards the yacht club.

Gina stopped and removed her phone from her pocket to ring John. He answered quickly.

"I've found her, by the river. I thought I might."

The conversation was brief. She slipped the phone back into her pocket and set off again. When she sat down next to Lili, she said nothing initially.

She could see now that she was crying silently, the tears obvious against her olive skin.

"It's a year today," Liliana whispered.

"It is. I'm sorry I got upset with you. I suppose I felt, well, that . . ."

"That the pasta sauce was the last bit of evidence that Papa existed?"

"Something like that. It was like he was still around, standing in the kitchen, his apron wrapped around him, singing Neapolitan songs."

Liliana took her mother's hand.

"He showed you how to make the sauce, didn't he?"

"Yes. But it never tastes the same when I make it. There's something missing. I think Papa had more patience than me. He used to let it simmer for hours."

Liliana pulled herself up.

"Well, there's something I need to tell you."

What now, Gina thought.

"Go on then, spit it out.'

Liliana opened her mouth to speak, but it froze there as she looked up the road towards the pier. Gina twisted round to see what had taken her attention. John and Dante were hurrying down the road.

"Might as well tell everyone at once," Liliana said. "Even better, Luca can help me."

It was then Gina noticed a familiar figure jogging across the road, the hem of one of Papa's aprons flapping as he went. Her cousin reached them as John and Dante did.

"Has Lili told you?' he said.

"Hadn't quite got around to it yet."

"It was really strange, Lili calling round this morning with her idea, because I was about to give you a ring.

"I was rooting around that big old freezer in the cellar, and what should I find shoved at the back?"

"Papa's pasta sauce!" the family chanted in unison.

"Yeah, six pots of Uncle Joe's special recipe, and it couldn't have been made long before he passed away."

"How wonderful!" Gina exclaimed, feeling the tears sting her eyes once more, this time in happiness.

"When Lili arrived and told me what had happened, we hatched a plan." He pointed to her to carry on.

"Luca's closed on Sunday evenings so we thought tomorrow we could have a dinner here, invite some of the family round."

"A celebration of Uncle Joe's life," Luca said. "Get Mama, Auntie Chiara, Uncle Marco, my brother and some of the cousins. But only if it's OK with you."

"Oh, yes, please, that's a great idea," Gina said.

"I'll make some fresh pasta, buy some good lamb from the butcher, crack open a couple of bottles of Gavi di Gavi.

"I just wish my tomato pasta sauce was as good as Uncle Joe's was. His was always the best." Luca put his hand sideways against his mouth. "But don't tell Mama I said that!"

Gina elbowed him playfully and the others laughed.

"Now, if you'll excuse me, I better get ready for opening." He looked up and down the road before almost skipping back to the restaurant.

John considered his family.

"What shall we do with the pot of sauce at home?"

"Have it this evening," Dante said.

"Papa's pasta sauce two evenings running?" Gina said. "Do we mind?"

"No!" came the resounding reply.

"What I thought."

They headed off, arm in arm, back down towards the pier. Gina and the children belted out a rendition of "O Sole Mio".

It was a song they'd all heard Papa sing since they were little, playing the conventional Neapolitan for customers and family alike.

Gina felt the happiest she had since her father had passed on.

She knew now he'd always be around her, in her children, in her aunts, uncle and cousins. In lots of their memories. And in all their attempts at his recipes – especially his pasta sauce. ∎

Shutterstock.

Erddig Hall, Wrexham

One of the finest features of this property is its collection of portraits. The Dining Room is festooned with pictures of previous owners of Erddig Hall, the Grade I listed building in Wrexham.

The Hall dates back to 1684, when it was designed by Thomas Webb for Joshua Edisbury, the High Sheriff of Denbighshire.

However, this ambitiously grand stately home bankrupted Edisbury.

John Meller, a London lawyer, took over the building set in acres of lush land and added to the property with two-storey wings, while lavishly furnishing the house, which was bequeathed to his nephew, Simon Yorke I.

All subsequent owners have either been called Simon or Philip, and the grand home remained in the Yorke family right up until the National Trust took ownership in 1973.

The Trust began restoring the house — which was sinking due to aged coal mine workings — and "lost" gardens were also restored.

The last Yorke's request was that nothing be removed from the house, so it is a treasure trove of antiquities from historic wallpaper through to portraits of the staff who were held in high regard.

One interesting fact about the Yorkes is that many were vegetarians, with five-year-old Philip Yorke I beginning the "tradition" in 1748.

There For Each Other

— by Andrea Wotherspoon —

M AYBE Heidi will open up to you," Kate said to her sister, Erin. "I just can't get through to her. These last few months, she's either been sullen and silent, or screaming the house down. She's been like that since Dad's memory really started going downhill, and now that he's moved into the home, she's even worse.

"She won't talk about what's happening, and she snaps my head off if I mention it."

"Poor Heidi. She was so close to Dad; no wonder she's struggling," Erin replied.

"I mean, it's typical teenage behaviour, to a point. But she's never been this bad before. She's fourteen, and old enough to understand what's happening, but still, she misses her grandad.

"Ignoring the situation doesn't help, though. We're all having to get used to it, and it's hard enough without constantly worrying about her."

Erin nodded.

"Well, I'll do my best. At least she's agreed to come for a walk with me. She wants to go out to St Mary's Chapel."

*　*　*　*

Erin and Kate's dad had finally been admitted to a residential home just a few weeks ago. His dementia had reached the stage where he could no longer live on his own, and although they could visit him regularly, he rarely remembered who they were.

The whole family was still coming to terms with things, but it had hit Heidi — his only granddaughter — hardest of all.

She was silent during the short drive out of town with Erin, spending most of it on her phone. Erin left her to it; maybe she would be chattier once they got to the chapel.

She wasn't sullen with Erin, like she was being with her mother; she

Illustration by Kirk Houston.

was just reluctant to engage in conversation. She smiled and replied politely, but she was distant.

They arrived in the small car park at the end of a farm track, and Erin was pleased to see there was no-one else there.

They climbed over the gate and set off the short distance through farmland along the coast, towards the ruins of St Mary's Chapel.

It was a pleasant October afternoon; the sky was clear, with just a light breeze coming from the north. They walked in silence, watched by inquisitive sheep.

"It's easy to picture Viking longboats heading for the coast here, isn't it?" Erin said, gesturing to the horizon.

She could clearly imagine them descending upon the unforgiving coastline, cutting through the volatile expanse of the sea as they would have done many hundreds of years ago.

"Yeah," was all Heidi said in response.

They crossed a bridge over a fast-flowing stream, then climbed up a steep path as the sound of the gushing stream gave way to roars of unseen waves crashing against the cliffs far below them.

Straight in front stood the ancient ruined building, a wall surrounding the tiny cemetery beside it. Beyond the rugged shoreline, the sea was a mix of gunmetal grey and frothy white.

"The chapel's been here about nine hundred years," Erin said. "There used to be an Iron Age broch here, too."

Heidi nodded and looked away.

"Grandad said it fell into the sea," she mumbled.

"Yes, the cliffs have eroded over the last couple of thousand years."

"They weren't here last time I was here," Heidi said, pointing towards three wind turbines a few fields away from the chapel.

"First there was a broch here, then a chapel and now electricity, so it's like each millennium humans are trying something different."

Erin smiled. Heidi could be very perceptive, and this was the most she had spoken since they'd left the house.

"That's a lovely way of looking at it. It's a spot our ancestors have used over the centuries, for whatever was important to them – religion, home, protection, renewable energy.

"It's a bit like looking at a cross-section of Caithness life through the ages."

They walked over to the roofless chapel.

"The church had a nave and a separate square-shaped chancel, more like contemporary Orcadian and Scandanavian churches, rather than like other Highland churches," Heidi said, reading from the information board. She wrinkled her nose. "I don't even know what a nave or chancel is."

"Didn't Grandad ever tell you?" Erin asked cautiously.

Heidi shrugged.

"Probably. But I've forgotten." She headed into the graveyard, followed by Erin.

The atmosphere inside the walls was one of sanctuary and protection, after feeling so exposed to the elements out on the clifftop.

Babysitting

I've spent the day with Theo; he's seven and a bit,
And just disproved illusions that I'm still young and fit.
This morning we were pirates, sailing stormy seas,
Till time for pirate victuals of fishcake, chips and peas.
And when we'd read a story of lands where monsters roam,
We baked a cake for Mummy to welcome her back home.
The kitchen's now chaotic, and I look old and grey,
Yet still I must confess it – it's been a brilliant day!

Maggie Ingall

There weren't a lot of gravestones, so they walked around, looking at the names and stories. Erin was hopeful that she could get Heidi to open up; she just needed to handle it carefully.

As she wandered amongst the stones, something caught her eye. Ladybirds. Six of them, huddled together in the curve on the side of a gravestone. Their red-spotted backs gleamed as if they had been polished.

"Heidi!" She gestured to her niece. "Come and see this!"

"Wow! I've never seen more than one ladybird in one go," Heidi said, holding her phone in front of the insects and taking a photograph. "Do you think they're hibernating or something?"

"I'm not sure. I guess it's the time of year for it," Erin said. As she peered at the tiny creatures, a memory came to her. "Hey, did Grandad ever tell you the story of how ladybirds got their name?"

Heidi hesitated for a moment, then rolled her eyes.

"Yeah, he said that there was a farmer out at John O' Groats, and all his crops were being eaten by aphids.

"So he prayed to the Virgin Mary, who sent loads of red insects with black spots down from heaven which ate all the aphids and saved the crops. So the farmer named them ladybirds after the Virgin Mary."

Erin laughed.

"He told us that one, too, when we were little. I had a feeling you would have heard it as well."

Heidi opened her mouth as if to say something, but then she paused and stared at a different gravestone.

"Oh, my goodness! There's loads of them on this one."

They counted a whopping twenty-one ladybirds on the second gravestone. By the time they had checked the other gravestones, they had counted almost a hundred throughout the cemetery.

"I wonder if there's a collective noun for ladybirds," Erin said. "A flock? A herd? A murder?"

"A murder?"

"A murder of crows. Honestly."

Heidi rolled her eyes.

"That sounds like one of Grandad's stories," she muttered, as she tapped away on her phone. "Oh, wow! You'll never believe this!" She beamed as she looked at Erin.

"What?"

"A group of ladybirds? Get this, it's called a loveliness. A loveliness of ladybirds."

"That's beautiful," Erin said, crouching down to look at them again.

"Yeah, it says here that they all huddle together over the winter, so that they can help keep each other safe from predators and bad weather. Isn't it sweet how they look out for each other?"

"It is," Erin replied. "They're not unlike humans in that respect."

Heidi frowned questioningly.

"We come together to help us get through hard times," Erin went on. "Like Grandad's illness."

Heidi looked away.

"I know it's horrible, and it's hard for all of us to see him like that. But we can support each other. And share our memories. Like his dodgy ladybird story."

Heidi kept her gaze averted, but Erin could see the smile. Then she turned back, her face solemn again.

"He's not going to get better though, is he?"

Erin shook her head.

"Not all ladybirds make it through the winter. But he's here now, and that's what matters. He doesn't always remember who we are, but we remember him, and we're there for each other.

"Don't feel that you can't talk about him, or talk about how you're feeling."

"I don't want to upset Mum," Heidi replied, looking stricken. "He's her dad, so it must be much worse for her."

Erin put an arm around her niece.

"There's no league table of who loves him the most. Your feelings are just as valid as your mum's, or mine, or anyone else's."

Heidi looked up her and smiled.

"We can form our own loveliness," she said. Erin smiled back.

"We absolutely can. Come on, let's go home. You can show your mum those photos. And ask her if she remembers how the ladybirds got their name." ■

Tennyson Down, Isle Of Wight

Victorian celebrity-spotters visiting the Isle of Wight might have spotted a figure striding across the chalk ridge that now bears his name. Poet Laureate Alfred, Lord Tennyson, lived at Freshwater Bay and described the bracing sea air as worth "sixpence a pint".

Now owned and managed by the National Trust, the Down is grazed by cattle and rabbits, which keep the turf short and springy.

The Down forms the western end of the Tennyson Heritage Coast and is part of the island's Area of Outstanding Natural Beauty and, with Headon Warren and West High Down, a Site of Special Scientific Interest (SSSI).

At the highest point of the West Wight chalk cliffs, the Tennyson Monument stands on the Down, some 147 m (482 ft) above sea level, the summit of a challenging hike for visitors.

The rewarding views no doubt helped when a national poll rated Tennyson Down as the fourth best place in Britain to have a picnic!

Coming Home

by Jessma Carter

I T always felt like coming home, although she had never lived there. Jennifer walked slowly up the path towards the bungalow door. It was still the same bright blue with a well-polished brass letter-box. She could almost see her grandma fiercely rubbing it, standing back to check the shine then giving a last flick with the duster.

"It's as well to keep it polished for you never know who's coming to the door or what's going to come through that letter-box."

Jennifer's gran, Doreen, was always prepared.

She seemed never to run out of sugar, eggs or flour. She was never caught out when a caller came, for her tins always held something home-made and there was always a kettle near boiling point.

Her home, she said with pride, was her castle, and it was up to her to keep order.

It had been summer when Jennifer had last visited her gran; now it was October and she was seeking refuge.

"Come away in," Doreen said, making no reference to Jennifer's unexpected arrival. "I'll just put a match to the fire, for there's a nip in the air."

It was only after Doreen bustled in with the tea tray and they were both settled by the fire that she finally turned to her granddaughter.

"What's ado then, lassie? I can see by your face there's something amiss."

Jennifer had to smile, for it was so like her gran to get straight to the point.

"It's a man, is it? That one you met at university last year? Is it him that's giving you grief?"

Of course, it was Donald that was giving her grief. Doreen was right, as usual.

Jennifer had always felt able to talk freely with her gran. Her mum and dad had moved to Italy when they were first married and Jennifer had

had a wonderful early childhood.

She attended an English-speaking school from the age of six, but later, her parents decided to send her to a boarding school in Scotland. She saw her grandmother nearly every weekend and spent the holidays with her parents.

Jennifer was unaware of anything unusual in her upbringing, for many of her friends at school had parents who worked abroad; many envied her having a grandmother whom she could visit and even take a friend to see on weekend afternoons.

"Yes," Jennifer said, "it's Donald. The trouble is, he plans everything for our lives. Everything for mine!

"We'll get married in two years. He'll take more exams and earn promotion. I can find what he calls an unstressful job. Whatever that is! And then we can start a family.

"That's his plan!"

"Does he know where you'll live?"

"He thinks somewhere in Edinburgh would be good. Perhaps a small flat to begin with."

Doreen laughed.

"Has he chosen the wallpaper yet?"

"Grandma!" Jennifer began to cry and laugh at the same time. "I need time away from him. Time to think."

"Let's have tea and talk," Doreen said. "I've got to go to a concert tonight, but you can stay in if you want. I'll be back as early as I can but I'm on the committee so I'm obliged to go.

"We're raising money for the local playgroup." She looked at Jennifer's tear-stained face. "Perhaps you'd like to come?"

Jennifer wiped away her tears.

"OK. Anything's better than sitting here moping." She managed a smile.

*   *   *   *

Jennifer immediately felt comfortable as she took her seat in the hall.

While Doreen was behind the scenes organising drinks and snacks for the post-concert get-together, she was free to sit down and have a look around.

Most of the audience were young women, leaning over towards one another, chatting, waving, settling themselves into their seats. The rest of the audience seemed to consist of school-age children and elderly people.

"How are you, Jennifer?" It was a hearty greeting from the man who leaned over her.

"You don't mind if I sit beside you? I'll just put my jacket on this seat for your gran when she's ready." Kenny Mitchell's eyes twinkled.

"I'm fair looking forward to this. Stop me if I join in the songs, will you? I get sorely tempted and my voice is no' just what it should be."

Jennifer began to think what a good idea it was for her to come. Kenny had been a neighbour and friend of her grandfather when he was alive.

Since she had first known him, everything about Kenny had been "no' as it should be."

His feet, so he said, took him in the wrong direction, his memory was "on the blink" and his stomach was "aye grumbling", but his face was always smiling and his hands there to help.

Just as the councillor was about to welcome everyone to the concert, Doreen, breathing hard after her efforts in the kitchen, slid into the seat beside Jennifer and leaned across to nod to Kenny.

It was difficult during the concert for Jennifer not to think of the evenings she had spent with her mother and father and brother back in Italy.

There, they had often had meals in restaurants where large families gathered, where there was shouting and singing and people moving from table to table to talk to their friends.

Here, it wasn't much different. Schoolchildren changed seats, stood up, got excited and pointed if they recognised someone on the stage, while the rest of the audience turned to nod to one another when one of their family was performing.

It was good to sit in the happy atmosphere.

Jennifer's doubts dissolved. For a weekend she would free herself from decision-making.

*   *   *   *

But Jennifer was shocked next morning at breakfast.

Doreen was giving the teapot a shake before pouring them a second cup.

"I'm going into hospital in two weeks for an operation to my knee."

144

She saw Jennifer's face. "I saw no need to tell anybody.
"It's my knee and my problem and I'm only telling you now because
you're here. Somebody might mention it and I wouldn't like you to be
surprised."
"What's wrong?"
"It's nothing much and there's no cause for you to go worrying about
t. It's not a big operation.
"It's what they call a cartilage that's twisted. I'll be right as rain in two
or three weeks."
Jennifer sat silently.
Grandma had always been there. She boasted that she never so much
as had a cold. She had always bustled around cooking and preparing
when Jennifer's family came back from Italy.
She had looked after Jennifer many weekends; she had welcomed her
friends and she, Jennifer, had never noticed that her gran was grimacing
a bit as she walked, that she had held tight on to Kenny's arm as they
walked home the night before.
She had been too wrapped up in her own affairs to notice, but now,
she could recall the way her gran had sat down with a sigh of relief as
soon as they had come home.
"It's all right, Kenny will call in every morning. He knows I'd do the
same for him," Doreen said briskly.
"Now, let's plan what we do today. We have all weekend to talk if need
be."

∗ ∗ ∗ ∗

"I've been thinking," Doreen said after the table had been cleared.
"Your chap Donald has never seen you with your family. It's no bad thing
to see people in their own patch. How about you asking him down here
for a weekend?"
Jennifer nodded.
"I've thought about that, Gran. Maybe I should. I've never met his
family, either. His father came from Stirling but Donald had all his
schooling in England."
"And what kind of feeling did you get when Donald spoke about his
folks?"
"He seemed fond of them, I suppose," Jennifer said. "He has two
young sisters, both still at school.
"I'll talk to Donald about it, see if he has a weekend spare – he plays
in a cricket team.
"In any case, I'll be here before you have your operation. We can talk
about it then."

∗ ∗ ∗ ∗

But just a few days after Jennifer went back to work, she had a phone
call from Kenny.
"Jennifer. Your gran's all right. That's the first thing I have to say.
"She's had her operation. She's fine. Someone cancelled and she was

taken in right away. Probably for the best, for it didn't give her time to fret.

"I've been to see her. She's fine and the surgeon is pleased with the way the operation went but she'll be laid up for a bit."

Jennifer breathed a sigh of relief.

"I'll be down on Friday, Kenny. I'll make sure everything's in order for her when she gets back home."

"She'll be glad to see you, Jennifer." She could hear the relief in his voice, too.

The following Friday evening, Jennifer arrived at the station. Kenny met her and made no comment on her red-rimmed eyes beyond reassuring her.

"Your gran's her old self. She'll be home this weekend. Everything's arranged.

"She'll have a nurse come to see her regular and I've given the hospital my number if anything untoward should happen. Just you get yourself a good sleep. I've seen to the heating so you'll be fine and cosy."

Jenny mumbled her thanks as Kenny fussed around her when they arrived at Gran's house, but she was glad to see him shuffle past the window towards his own house.

It wasn't just her grandmother being ill that had upset her. It was Donald's reaction.

"Jenny. This weekend! Again! There's no cricket match this weekend so I'm free. I assumed we could see each other.

"I had planned that we could go for a good long walk up the hill and then have a meal out at the Eagle Inn."

There had been shouting and tears and two people unable to communicate. There had been things said that would be difficult to unsay.

Jennifer had tried to explain that her gran had always been there when her parents were abroad. He had always had his parents around, looking after their precious boy.

Donald had accused her of selfishness, of not understanding his needs. Had he now to rearrange his whole weekend?

He had had an offer to join a group on an outing to Loch Lomond and he had turned it down!

"Just listen to yourself," Jennifer had said. "All you care about is you."

The train journey had been miserable. She had kept hoping that maybe Donald would rush down to the station in the morning, that he would be waiting for her on the platform, that they could apologise to one another.

But there was no sign of Donald on the grey morning platform.

Perhaps this unexpected weekend would help her to make a decision about him.

* * * *

Gran was ready for them — she was sitting dressed and in a wheel-chair beside her bed in the ward. She looked well and dismissed any questions about how she felt.

"Just get me out of here," she said as she let Jennifer kiss her on the cheek and held out her hand to be caught in a fierce grip by Kenny.

"You're looking no' too bad." Kenny was at his most complimentary, while his face shone with pleasure.

"I'm no' bad at all," Doreen answered, "although I could do with one of your cups of tea, Kenny.

"The nurses are good, very kind, but they make awful strong tea. They're no' all that quick at taking out the bags."

Jennifer smiled at their easy familiarity. It was good that her gran had such a good neighbour.

Soon, they were settled in the taxi.

"Ask the driver to go by the sea, Kenny," Doreen said as they settled her in the taxi.

"Kenny knows I don't like to be confined," she said to Jennifer. "He knows how I hated being in hospital."

Jennifer understood her gran's desire to go by the sea on the way home. There was something for ever about the sea.

It was always there, in different moods, different colours, but always there. They were quiet in the taxi, all three of them engaged in peaceful thought.

$$* \quad * \quad * \quad *$$

After they had had a meal prepared by Kenny, a nurse called at the house to help Doreen get settled for the night.

Kenny went back to his own home, promising to return in the morning and urging them both to give him a ring if they needed any help before then.

Gran gave a sigh.

"Only me and you now, Jenny. Thank goodness for that. There's only so much fussing I can stand." She lay back on her pillow and reached out for Jennifer's hand.

"Tell me then. What's ado with you and Donald?" She shook her head. "I can see there's something on your mind."

Jennifer told her, relieved to have someone to listen.

"He's young yet, Jenny. I can see he's important to you and you're not quite sure if you're important to him."

They sat together silently for a while.

Doreen was the first to speak.

"You know, your grandpa was never much of a one for words.

"We went out walking together for months and to be perfectly honest with you I was getting a bit weary waiting for him to speak up about his feelings.

"One Saturday I said I was going with my best friend Bessie for a trip to see her mother and I'd no' be able to see him on Sunday."

Doreen smiled.

"That got him going! He looked so surprised. Not disappointed or anything. Surprised. He'd taken it for granted, you see, that I would be there every Sunday.

"Maybe your Donald was surprised."

"So Grandpa told you how he felt, and asked you to marry him?" Jennifer asked.

"Nothing of the sort. I said I was free to go where I wanted, free as a bird."

"And then?"

"Then it took him a whole twenty-four hours before he called on me saying he was sure I knew how he felt for why else was he taking me out every Sunday?

"So I asked him to tell me how he felt," Doreen went on.

"And?"

"Well, he stumbled and stuttered and then came out with it. I like you, he said. In fact, if the truth be known, I can't think of living without you. I love you!" Doreen was smiling at the memory.

"Say it again, I said. Do you know what he answered? He said, once is enough." Doreen laughed.

She took hold of Jennifer's hand.

"Some people are not much good at saying what they feel. Donald has planned a life together with you.

"He was maybe just a bit disappointed that you wouldn't be there for him this weekend, and it came out wrong. And then you thought of all the other things he had said that annoyed you."

Kenny knocked and popped his head round the kitchen door.

"Anything I can do, ladies?"

"Not just now, thanks, Kenny," Doreen replied.

She waited until he left and then turned to Jennifer.

"You can see, and I know, he's fond of me. He doesn't need to say. Friends don't need to say.

"But passion complicates so much and it's difficult to deal with when you're young."

Jennifer's phone rang and she went to pick it up from the table.

"Jenny, I'm sorry, I'm sorry. I was disappointed that you weren't free." There was a pause while Jennifer listened for more.

"Jenny. Jenny? Are you there?" Donald sounded almost afraid.

"Yes. I'm with my gran. She's been in hospital."

There was silence for several seconds.

"I can't come, then?" Donald asked.

"Maybe you can come once Gran is fitter. I'd like you two to meet." Jennifer had to try to sound decisive.

"I'll let you know when I'm coming back to my flat, but I'm staying here for a week at least, and Gran's not ready for visitors yet."

Jennifer put down the phone and looked at her gran. They sat together silently for a while until Doreen spoke.

"It'll do him no harm to wait. And it would do you no harm, either. What's for you will no' go by you."

Jennifer laughed.

As usual, Gran was right. They had all the time in the world. ■

Shutterstock.

Callendar House

Callendar House in Falkirk is steeped in history, dating back centuries. In fact, part of the embankment is a section of the Antonine Wall, built 2,000 years ago by the Romans.

Over the centuries, Callendar House has hosted such historical figures as Mary, Queen of Scots, Cardinal Beaton, John Knox, Oliver Cromwell, Bonnie Prince Charlie and Queen Victoria.

Over the years, the house has been redesigned and expanded. In the 19th century it was styled after a French Renaissance chateau.

The interiors were restored to their former Georgian style, including the kitchen's bread oven. The Morning Room is opulent and the oak-panelled library houses Falkirk Archives.

The Forbes family resided here until Falkirk Burgh bought the building in 1962.

Callendar House is set in 170 acres, which includes woodland, an arboretum and ornamental gardens, as well as a mausoleum. Callendar Park is listed as a historically important designed landscape.

Sweet Memories

by Pamela Wray

L IKE her mother before her, Miss Mabel Trot kept the corner shop on our street. The old lady was a friend of my mum's, and I called her Aunt Mabel.

The back parlour of her shop was old-fashioned and seemed to hold a secret sadness.

A grandfather clock ticked in the shadows, a chenille cloth hid the table legs, and a sepia photograph on the mantelpiece showed a young Aunt Mabel, her hair loose around her shoulders, standing beside a handsome soldier.

And on the sideboard, there was always a little sealed glass jar of Bonfire Toffee.

Each year, for the fifth of November, Aunt Mabel kept up the tradition of making Bonfire Toffee. She made mountains of it and sold it in the shop. It was the best I ever tasted.

However, when I was nine years old, disaster struck.

In the October, just before she started her toffee-making marathon, she called at our house.

"This is for you, Jilly," she said, presenting me with the jar of Bonfire Toffee from her sideboard, as she did every year.

"Thank you, Aunt Mabel," I said, delighted.

"You're welcome." She smiled.

But as she turned to leave, she tripped over Tiddles, our over-friendly cat, who had twined himself around her legs, and she fell heavily on the path, with her right arm twisted underneath her.

"Oh, no!" I cried, rushing to help. Mum rushed out, too. And Tiddles fled under the hedge.

Poor Aunt Mabel. She had sprained her wrist.

Mortified, Mum couldn't apologise enough and promised that she would help out in the shop whenever she could.

She also offered to take on the mammoth task of making the Bonfire

Illustration by Jim Dewar.

Toffee for Aunt Mabel, and asked me if I would like to help.

Of course I would! I couldn't wait to see what went into it and learn how to make it. I could make some any time I liked then, couldn't I? Not just at bonfire time.

Trouble was, the recipe turned out to be a family secret that Aunt Mabel wouldn't part with.

Mum and I went into a huddle. How could we persuade Aunt Mabel to give us the recipe so that we could make the toffee for her, and she could keep up the tradition?

We came up with some good reasons and trotted off to the shop to try to talk her round.

Nobody was waiting to be served and Aunt Mabel was leaning glumly against the bacon slicer.

She greeted us with a big smile.

"Oh, how nice to see you. Please come through. I'll put the kettle on." And she lifted the flap in the counter, and ushered us into the back parlour.

Aunt Mabel gave me a glass of milk and opened her well-stocked biscuit tin.

"Help yourself."

Mum made a pot of tea for the two of them, and brought it through on a pretty tray and set it down on the chenille cloth.

After Mum had drained her cup, she got down to the business of the toffee-making.

"Let's face it, Mabel," she began. "With the best will in the world, you can't possibly make the Bonfire Toffee this year, can you? Not with your stirring arm all strapped up like that."

Aunt Mabel cradled her poorly arm.

"No, for the first time ever, I can't." She sighed.

"And if your famous Bonfire Toffee doesn't get made," Mum continued, "you're going to disappoint an awful lot of customers, aren't you? And not just your regulars.

"What about all those other people who come from miles around especially to buy your toffee? And then they usually buy lots of other things in the shop at the same time, don't they, and boost your takings?"

Aunt Mabel nodded.

"Yes, you're quite right about the customers and the takings."

"So why don't you just let Jilly and me make it for you, then? We'd really like to help, you know."

"You're very kind." Aunt Mabel put her cup down and patted Mum's hand. "And please don't think I don't appreciate your offer. Truly, I do.

"But you see, the recipe has always been kept within the family before. And the making of it for sale in the shop, rather than just for the family, was only a tradition started in my mother's day, and there's something else about the recipe . . ." She tailed off.

What else? I was intrigued. Was Aunt Mabel hinting at secret ingredients? How exciting.

No more details were forthcoming.

But the upshot was that after Mum had solemnly sworn that she would never show the recipe to another living soul, Aunt Mabel relented and handed it over.

And Mum slid the folded piece of paper into her pocket before I got the teeniest glimpse of it.

*   *   *   *

On the day of the toffee-making, I got up really early and dashed downstairs to the kitchen. But Mum was there ahead of me and she had already mixed up all the ingredients, so I didn't get a chance to see what went into it.

I looked around for the hush-hush recipe, expecting to see a well-thumbed, toffee-stained piece of paper covered in spidery writing. But no such thing was anywhere in sight. Clearly, Mum was going to keep the recipe a secret from me.

After we had eaten our breakfast – porridge with honey for Mum, a dippy egg with soldiers for me, and mashed-up tuna for Tiddles – Mum banished Tiddles from the kitchen for the sake of hygiene, and in case he got under our feet, and lit the gas rings under the three huge, heavy-based saucepans on top of the stove.

"I'll be in charge of two of the pans, Jilly," she said. "And you'll be in charge of the third."

Eagerly, I scrubbed my hands. Mum tied my hair back into a ponytail and pinnied me up, and I climbed on to a low stool by the hob.

Armed with a large wooden spoon, and feeling very grown up, I

Fireworks Night

The night sky is lit in colours so bright,
Red, green and purple, orange and white,
Skyrockets whistle, soar up to the moon
Then they erupt, a dazzling monsoon,
Explosions of gunpowder crack through the dark,
A cascade of fire drops, light beams and sparks,
Fizgigs and bangers, Catherine wheels, too,
Fountains and pinwheels of pink, gold and blue,
The crowd oohs and aahs at every new sight,
A once-a-year treat, it's Fireworks Night!

Lily Christie

started stirring the dark liquid in the pan in front of me.

I was in heaven, swooning in the wondrous heady smell of the warming mix, and trying not to drool.

Soon it reached a seething boil and whooshed up in the pan.

"Be careful, Jilly, it's dangerous, hot stuff," Mum warned, a slightly worried look on her face.

"And could you please stir it in figures of eight, dear? Not round and round. And do make sure it doesn't catch and burn at the bottom."

I stirred vigorously, on and on, getting hotter and hotter, and when my arm was just about to fall off, Mum said I could stop.

"Right, it's time to turn the heat down and see if the toffee's reached setting point."

Shutterstock.

153

She dropped a heaped teaspoonful of the hot mix into a cup of cold water and squished the blob between her fingers.

"Yes, it's done," she said, as the toffee hardened up.

"And now for the taste test." Mum passed the blob over to me.

It was a lovely big gobstopper of a blob. I sniffed and licked it, popped it into my mouth and rolled it round and round with my tongue.

I sucked it, and shut my eyes and sucked it some more, slowly relishing the sweet treacly flavours and dribbly lusciousness. Sheer bliss.

When I had sucked the blob down to the size of a small pebble, I crunched it, so that the sticky crumbs of toffee would cling around my teeth and the gorgeousness would stay in my mouth for a bit longer.

"That was absolutely delicious," I managed to say at last. "And do you know what, Mum, it tastes even better than last year's," I added, already craving some more.

"Oh, good!" She grinned.

On the kitchen side was a row of oiled and lined tin trays. Mum heaved the heavy pans over to the trays and carefully poured the molten toffee into them until the bases were generously covered with the rich, dark mixture.

We left the glossy sheets of toffee to cool for the rest of the morning.

After a sandwich lunch, Mum checked on the row of trays and declared that the toffee was ready for the next stage.

"It's time to smash it up, Jilly," she said, handing me a little toffee hammer.

Immediately, I bashed a tray enthusiastically. Shards of toffee flew everywhere.

"Not into smithereens, love." Mum laughed. "Just into bite-sized chunks."

Mum whacked the toffee in the other trays with her rolling pin.

Once we had broken up all the gleaming sheets, we started wrapping the bite-sized chunks in little squares of greaseproof paper. Mum smiled wryly, as I popped yet another piece of the irresistible toffee into my mouth.

"Don't eat any more, Jilly," she said. "You'll make yourself sick. And just in case you're tempted again, dear, you must whistle while you work.

"It's not possible to whistle and eat toffee at the same time. And don't worry," she added with a twinkle, as my face fell. "There'll be plenty left for you in the trays at the end."

So I whistled and worked alongside Mum until we had filled 10 tall glass sweet-jars with the neatly wrapped chunks of our very first batch of Bonfire Toffee.

Aunt Mabel was thrilled when we took the jars round to the shop. She stood them in prime position in the window for everyone to see.

I felt very proud to see them there, knowing I had helped to make them. And it felt good to have helped her to keep up the tradition when she wouldn't have managed on her own.

In next to no time, the toffee had all sold out and we had to boil up another batch, and we made several more after that. It seemed as if people just couldn't get enough of it.

∗　∗　∗　∗

For years afterwards, Mum and I helped Aunt Mabel make the Bonfire Toffee, although Mum still kept the recipe a secret from me.

Until the day she got careless, and I spied it sticking out from under the cutlery drawer. And, yes, of course, I read it!

The recipe called for Blackstrap Molasses, golden syrup and dark brown sugar, butter, white wine vinegar and cream of tartar.

Nothing seemed particularly secret about the ingredients, except for the Blackstrap Molasses, which I had never heard of before.

However, written along the bottom of the recipe in tiny writing, in a quite different script from the rest of it, was the following message: *Please keep some for Tom.*

I confronted Mum, brandishing the recipe.

"Who's Tom? And what's the message about?"

"Ah, you found it." She grinned. "I'm sorry I had to hide the recipe from you, love, but I'd made that promise to Mabel."

"Anyway, I reckon you've earned the right to know about it now, what with all the toffee you've helped me to make for her."

She took the recipe from me and smoothed it out on the kitchen table, and we sat down next to each other.

"Well, dear," Mum said. "About Tom. Tom was Mabel's older brother. I never met him, but he's the soldier pictured with her in that photograph on the mantelpiece."

"Oh. I thought the handsome soldier was her boyfriend."

"No, he was Mabel's handsome brother."

"OK, well, why is he mentioned here, at the bottom of the recipe, in different writing?" I pointed to the message. "And why must they keep some toffee for him?"

"I wanted to know that, too, dear, when I first read the message. I saw it when we got home from Mabel's that day – the day she gave me the recipe.

"And while you were snuggled up with Tiddles on the sofa, watching 'Blue Peter' on the TV, I nipped back to the shop and asked Mabel about it, and she said her mother had written the message."

"Why did she write it?"

"Well, Tom was expected back home from the war that autumn, dear, and to celebrate his return, Mabel's mother made his favourite treat of Bonfire Toffee." Mum paused. "But Tom never came back."

"Do you mean he was killed in the war?"

"Yes, love." Mum sighed. "And afterwards, Mabel and her mother made Bonfire Toffee every autumn, and they always kept a little sealed jar of it on the sideboard, in Tom's memory."

"Oh, how sad," I said. "How very sad."

And suddenly I was moved to tears that Aunt Mabel always gave me Tom's special jar of Bonfire Toffee, every year. ■

Play The Game

by Enid Reece

TRADE is dropping," Pippa told Scott as she added up the day's takings. She looked around the café.

As soon as they had viewed it, they'd both decided it was just what they had been looking for and sunk all their savings into it.

"Something will turn up. It always does," he said, trying to reassure her. "At least we still have the lunchtime trade."

That was true, but now, with many of the shops closing in the high street after the out-of-town shopping mall opened, Pippa wondered how long that would last.

"Right, I'm off to the cash and carry," Scott said.

Pippa turned her attention to her daily routine. The smell of fresh coffee filtered through the air and she breathed in the aroma that was so familiar to her.

It had started to rain, big fat droplets making their way down the windows.

"Morning, Derek," she said as one of her regular customers came through the door half an hour later.

"Morning, Pippa. Nasty weather." He dropped his umbrella into the stand by the door and swept a hand through his thinning hair.

"Hopefully it won't last. The usual?" she asked but didn't wait for a reply.

Derek's preference never changed – a double espresso. She smiled as he took a sip and closed his eyes, enjoying the strong brew.

"Mmm. That's hit the spot." He looked around the café. "No Scott this morning?"

"Gone to the cash and carry. He'll be back soon. Don't worry, you can have your usual chat about football." She knew how much the pair liked to natter about their local team.

"If only that was all I wanted to chat about," he said, frowning.

He didn't look happy and Pippa raised an eyebrow.

Illustration by Kirk Houston.

"What's up?"

"The Rose and Crown, that's what's up," he said, scrubbing a hand over his weathered face. "It's closing."

"Oh, no." Pippa didn't like the sound of that at all. The pub had been situated in the high street for what seemed like for ever.

"Business that bad?" she asked.

Derek shook his head.

"Not that I noticed. The place has been sold. It's going to be turned into one of those gastro places. All mod cons."

"Maybe it's not a bad thing," Pippa said, thinking that at least it would bring customers back to the high street. Or more likely it would mean she would lose the office workers as they tried something different.

She kept her thoughts to herself. It was no good worrying about something that hadn't happened yet.

"Does that mean you'll have to find a new watering hole?" she said.

Derek said nothing for a moment and took another sip of his coffee.

"If that was the only problem I wouldn't mind."

"Oh?"

"It's the chess club." Derek nodded. "We meet once a week. A bit of a gossip and a game. We love it.

"Anyway, we meet up at the Rose and Crown every Tuesday. The landlord lets us use a small room at the side, away from the regulars."

"Seems a bit unsociable."

Derek shrugged.

"It's not a traditional pub game, like darts or dominoes. There's not much interaction."

Before she could ask anything more a woman with two children walked through the door and Pippa went to serve them.

Two hot chocolates and a coffee later, and Pippa went back to Derek.

"You were saying about the chess club?"

Derek pushed his empty mug towards her.

"Refill first, please."

"So, come on, what's the problem? Surely you can move to another pub?" she said once she'd refilled his mug.

"That's the problem. The days of pubs with separate rooms are long gone. I think the Rose and Crown was one of the last. Nowadays, there's one big room, or if there are two, the other one is used for functions."

"How about the community centre?"

Derek shook his head.

"First thing I thought of, but Tuesday afternoons it's booked for the local amateur dramatics."

"Couldn't you play on another day?"

"It suits us all to have it on that day. Some of them have other commitments for the rest of the week."

Pippa was about to say perhaps they could rearrange their busy lives when she heard raised voices and turned to see the two children arguing.

The mother looked up from the paperwork she was studying and told them to behave themselves. It didn't seem to do much good as one child pushed the other, sending the contents of a mug spilling over the table.

A quick reaction from the mother avoided the paperwork getting soaked.

"Back in a minute," Pippa said to Derek, grabbing a cloth and hurrying over to the woman, who was trying her best to mop up with a tissue.

"Here, let me," she said, wiping up the spilt drink.

The mother looked up, her face red.

"I'm so sorry. They're a bit restless, I'm afraid."

"Accidents happen," Pippa said, mopping away the last of the spillage.

"I was hoping they'd keep quiet while I filled this in." The woman tapped a form which lay in front of her. "I need to have it handed back in today."

The children began to squabble again and the mother folded the form in two.

"I think I'd better go before this turns into an all-out argument. They can get pretty noisy, I'm afraid."

Pippa looked around the café. There were no other customers and she didn't mind a bit of noise as long as it didn't get out of hand.

She turned to the children.

"How would you like to play a game of Hungry Hippos? I just so happen to have it under the counter."

"Oh, could we, Mum?" both children chorused, pleading eyes looking at their mother.

"Are you sure?" she said to Pippa.

"No problem. It'll keep them occupied while you finish with your paperwork."

A few minutes later, the children were having fun.

"Perhaps not the quietest of games," she said to Derek.

He peered over her shoulder and laughed.

"But they're enjoying it."

The door opened again and she could see Scott struggling with a couple of boxes. She went to help but Derek beat her to it, taking one of the boxes from Scott.

"Thanks, mate," he said, putting the box behind the counter and indicating for Derek to do the same.

"I see United did well at the weekend." He poured himself a mug of coffee.

"They certainly did," Derek agreed, "and about time, if you ask me."

The door opened again and Pippa left them to talk about their favourite subject as she served cups of coffee to a group of women.

The children were still enjoying the game and shouts of delight filled the café.

"Thanks. That was just what they needed," the mother said gratefully as she handed back the game half an hour later.

"Any time," Pippa assured her.

∗ ∗ ∗ ∗

Pippa sat with Scott, drinking their daily winding-down cup of coffee after the café had closed.

"Bad news about the Rose and Crown," Scott remarked as he helped himself to a chocolate biscuit. "I mean, I don't mind the upgrade, but sometimes it's good to see the charm of the old pubs with a separate bar and lounge.

"Pippa," he said, touching her arm when she didn't reply.

"Oh, sorry. I was thinking," she said. "Derek's little problem. Maybe we could help. The idea came to me when I saw those children playing the board game."

Scott looked puzzled.

"What on earth have the children got to do with Derek?"

"Just hear me out. How about we offer Derek and his mates a space here for the chess club?"

"Here?" Scott looked surprised.

"Why not? We have space," she said reasonably.

It was true; that was one of the things that had appealed to them when they viewed the business all those years ago.

"There's room to grow," was Scott's comment at the time.

"I suppose they could set up over there," he said, nodding towards four tables in the corner that wouldn't interfere with the everyday running of the café.

"My thinking exactly. I also had another thought."

"Go on."

"The children playing the game."

"It was a good idea at the time and they seemed to enjoy it."

She smiled.

"That's exactly what I thought. Usually, you see kids engrossed on the screen of their mobile."

"That's what the kids of today do," he agreed.

"When I looked at those kids today they were enjoying themselves – interacting." She shifted in her chair and grabbed hold of Scott's hand. "How about we buy a few more games? You could put up some shelves to display them and the children could try them out when they come in with their parents. What do you think?"

"How many games were you thinking of buying?"

She shrugged.

"Not that many. Just enough to see if the idea takes off. You know, a café with coffee, cakes and board games. Something a bit different. We could advertise. If it takes off, hopefully business will pick up."

Scott was dubious but had to agree that it was worth a try.

"OK, let's give it a go. What have we got to lose?"

*　*　*　*

Twelve months later, Pippa shut the door on the local press and looked around the busy café. Who would have thought that they'd be nominated for Business Initiative of the Year?

Her idea had worked. They'd started slowly with only a little interest, but soon the word spread and business picked up.

Even Derek was involved in the success when some of the older children began to watch the chess games and wanted to learn. There was now a children's chess club once a week.

"Another booking," Scott said, putting down the telephone as she approached the counter.

They'd branched out over the last couple of months, offering games evening for adults. The business was booming and they'd had to take on extra staff to cope.

"Great. By the way, love the outfit," she said, admiring his black and gold butterfly wings. There was a party going on in the corner and the children had wanted to dress up as different butterflies.

The Butterfly Farm was a board game whereby the children had to collect different butterflies, scoring higher points for the rarer ones found.

To make the children feel at home, Pippa and Scott had decided to join in the fun.

Scott chuckled.

"Do I get high points for being a monarch butterfly?"

"Probably," she said, laughing. "Although I doubt I'll get many myself, just being a humble cabbage white."

Pippa looked around the café. There was a group in the corner leafing through the book swap shelf, an idea of Scott's.

"Can you believe this started with a game of Hungry Hippos?" She turned back to Scott. "Fancy a game as a reminder after we close?"

"Why not?" he said over his shoulder as one of the children pulled him back to the game. She laughed and went to join him. ∎

Shutterstock.

The Argory, County Armagh

Built in the 1820s, this grand house has a 320-acre wood and beautiful sweeping gardens leading to riverside walks that bring a change of scenery with each season, from snowdrops through to an abundance of spring bulbs and a wildflower meadow.

There's also a two-mile wheelchair-friendly route that follows the pollarded lime trees walk.

The estate borders the River Blackwater, and it's easy to see why this house is often referred to as a jewel in the National Trust's crown!

The Greek revival villa was built for the McGeough-Bond family in the 1820s by architects John and Arthur Williamson.

It suffered fire damage in 1898, with the service wing being rebuilt.

It remains largely unchanged since the 1900s, with the owner leaving it to the National Trust in 1979, with much of his George IV furniture remaining.

The acetylene system of lighting is one of the most complete in the British Isles, and an original cast-iron ornamental solid-fuel-fired warm-air stove is just one example of its many features that highlight the technological changes through the decades.

The First Day Of Christmas

by Sally Winterflood

J O, I can't find the cat up here anywhere." My husband, Bob, sounds stressed.

"She can't have got out; we haven't opened the doors," I call back up the stairs. "Have you tried in the wardrobe? She might've sneaked in when I put the laundry away."

We are both devoted to our little black cat, Shadow, but she's totally neurotic, and seems to sense when something is about to happen to upset our normally quiet household.

And today being Christmas Day, with eight members of our family due to descend on us at any moment, she's gone into hiding.

"Found her!"

I hear the wardrobe door click shut, and within seconds, Shadow scoots past me into the sitting-room, back legs sliding on the newly exposed floorboards.

I've had to take up every rug in the house and clean the whole place to within an inch of its life, because Bob's sister, Helen, is coming, and she's allergic to cats.

So many preparations for just one day in the year. No, two, actually, because they're all staying over. The amount of towels and bedding I've had to sort out!

I even had to borrow a couple of air beds from my friend, Sue. I pumped those up first thing, and shoved them behind the sofa in the sitting-room, all ready for Helen and Josh, our teenage nephew.

Illustration by Shutterstock.

I've put Chloe and Rich in her old bedroom, Auntie Vi and Uncle Jack in Sophie's old room, and Sophie and Dan have got the sofa-bed in the little back room. Bodies everywhere!

It's taken some planning, but I'm confident I've got everything under control. The turkey's been in the oven since ten and everything else is prepped and ready. I do like to be organised.

My to-do list and cooking schedule are taped to the larder door for easy reference – it's all about the timing, today.

I have to confess, since they all confirmed they were coming, I've lost sleep most nights. I've been waking up to nip to the loo, getting back into bed and going into planning mode, lying there, creating lists in my head.

And it's not just been a question of where to sleep everyone, and which presents to buy, although that did give me a few headaches – it's been the matter of dietary allergies, intolerances and preferences.

You see, we're a really mixed bunch in terms of what we choose to, or can, eat. For weeks now, my culinary challenge has been uppermost in my mind.

In fact, I changed the words of "The Twelve Days Of Christmas" and it keeps playing over and over in my head.

"Four carnivores, three veggies, two gluten-free, and a vegan to top it all off . . ."

It's not that I mind, but trying to cook so many variations, and get them all on the table at the same time, is no mean feat. Thank goodness for my double oven.

The turkey and all the trimmings are straightforward enough, the nut roast, too, but the salmon's going to be tricky – horrible if it's overdone. The gluten-free gravy, the vegan gravy and the watercress sauce for the fish are ready. They just need zapping in the microwave to reheat, and I'll make the turkey gravy once I've carved.

"Can I do anything to help, love?" Bob potters into the kitchen with an "I'll offer, but hope she says no" look on his face.

I oblige.

"No thanks, all under control. Fingers crossed. Although, yes, maybe a sherry would be nice."

They'll be here soon. I should loosen up a bit – look as though this is all effortless.

"Of course, sherry, very Christmassy." He smiles as he pours me a glass. "All organised, Jo, as usual. We put on a good show, don't we?"

"We?"

"Turkey smells good already." He sniffs the air appreciatively, "Lovely, can't wait to have some with a good dollop of bread sauce."

Bread sauce! Please let there be a packet mix in the larder.

Fortunately, there is, and the near-disaster has been averted. I've made the bread sauce, and I won't let on that the use-by date was back in June.

"Oh, there's the phone. Can you get that, love?"

Bob reappears at the kitchen door with bad news.

"That was Dan, Sophie's not feeling too good. Stomach's a bit iffy, apparently. They're on their way, but she may not be up to lunch."

"Oh, no, not on Christmas Day. Poor thing."

There's a ring at the doorbell that sends the ever-scatty Shadow darting back upstairs. It's Auntie Vi and Uncle Jack. Vi, in her wheelchair, is barely visible beneath the bags of presents piled up on her lap.

Between them, Jack and Bob lift them all off, help Vi on to her sticks, and lead her into the sitting-room.

Next to arrive are Chloe, our youngest, and her husband, Rich, closely followed by Helen and Josh. Nearly all here now. Just waiting for Sophie and Dan.

Bob gets busy organising drinks for everyone and passing round the smoked salmon blinis.

"Is this salmon from a sustainable source, Uncle Bob?" Josh hesitates, awaiting an answer before committing himself.

"Well, it's organic, so I guess so. I thought you were vegetarian these days, though?"

"I am, but I still eat fish."

"That makes you a pescatarian, then." Chloe, who's a vegan, knows about these things.

"S'pose so." He shrugs, decides against the smoked salmon blini, and opts instead for a hummus and olive version.

There's another ring at the bell. I open the door to see two very pale faces looking back at me. With a hasty "Happy Christmas, Mum, sorry about —" both Sophie and Dan sprint up the stairs, leaving all their bags in a heap in the hallway.

We carry on and exchange our presents around the tree, minus the poorly pair, who have now fully succumbed to the vicious stomach bug that's doing the rounds and who are unlikely to reappear downstairs any time today.

Back in the kitchen again, I juggle pots, pans and ovens in a manner worthy of a "MasterChef" finalist. Once everything is ready, I call everyone to the table.

My trusty to-do list and cooking schedule have done me proud, and I'm thrilled to bits to have all permutations of Christmas lunch (or is it dinner?) arranged on platters and in lidded vegetable dishes on my electric hot-plates.

They're both laden with all the various options, and the pre-warmed plates are stacked at each end for people to help themselves.

I've removed Sophie and Dan's place settings and there's now a bit more elbow room for the remaining eight of us on our not-quite-large-enough kitchen table.

Even so, with the red candles lit, our best cutlery and wine glasses out, plus the crackers and tartan napkins, it all looks very festive, and I feel a real sense of achievement as I await the entrance of my hungry guests.

"Actually, where are they? Didn't they hear me call them?" I stomp along the hall and barge into the sitting-room, knocking a bauble off the Norwegian spruce, having temporarily forgotten that it's behind the door where the bookcase usually stands.

"Come on, you lot, it's ready."

A heated debate going on between Auntie Vi and Uncle Jack is holding everyone up. They always bicker, have done for as long as I can remember, but they seem properly locked in battle now.

And on Christmas Day! When my hard-won culinary victory has been dished up and is waiting to be eaten!

"I'm telling you, Vi, we've watched every single one." Jack, swirling the remains of his second pre-lunch whisky around his glass, presses the point. "Right from the very first year that she did it."

"Not today, you two, please. I want everything to be perfect."

Vi is adamant.

"No, we haven't. They first televised the Queen's speech in 1957. We didn't get a telly until 1962."

To break the deadlock I loudly order everyone to the table.

Chloe, ever the peace-maker, links arms with Jack, while Rich helps Vi on to her sticks, and they all shuffle into the kitchen.

* * * *

Well, it's half-three now, and if I say so myself, lunch was a triumph. And even though, without Sophie and Dan, we were one gluten-free and a veggie down, there's very little left over.

Apart, that is, from the extras I've already put aside for Boxing Day cold cuts and bubble-and-squeak. Our multiple-choice Christmas lunch turned out to be quite a jolly affair after all.

Vi and Jack soon got over their disagreement about the Queen's speech, and aside from Helen going into meltdown when she suddenly realised that Shadow was under her chair, and Josh dissecting his salmon in search of microscopic plastic particles, we had a fine time.

The table, scattered with the remains of pulled crackers, joke slips and plastic novelties, looks exactly as a post-Christmas lunch table should: red candles, burnt low but still flickering, the tablecloth dotted with drips of congealed gravy and custard, and here and there, crumbs of sage and onion stuffing and mince-pie pastry.

I see all the bread sauce was eaten – hopefully that's a good thing.

"Can somebody help me up, please, so I can pop to the loo?" Vi, her red paper crown slightly askew, wobbles her way along the passageway, accompanied by Rich on his way for a quick cigarette outside.

The second we realise Rich's intention and hear the door open, Bob and I both yell with one voice, "Cat!"

I know the family think we fuss too much about Shadow dashing out of the front door. It's Bob mainly. We're near a busy road, and he feels we need to keep her indoors.

As I'm pondering who's the most neurotic, Bob or the cat, the sudden sound of breaking glass, followed by loud expletives from Vi, sends me rushing towards the downstairs toilet.

"I'm all right, dear, really." She opens the door. "I'm so sorry. I knocked that little candle thingy off the shelf as I reached for the soap."

I'm dismayed to see the shattered remains of my favourite Christmas tealight holder lying at the bottom of the unforgiving ceramic basin. Luckily, she hasn't cut herself, so that's good.

"Don't worry, Vi," I say, picking up the broken glass and swilling the basin. "I never liked it that much anyway."

I steer her back to the kitchen, where I'm delighted to find that the table has been cleared, and the Monopoly board set up. Bob's topped up everybody's wine, and once I've sat down, he raises his glass.

"To Jo: thank you for working so hard to make this a truly wonderful, good old-fashioned family Christmas for us all."

So, it seems I managed it. A few issues along the way, but everyone's happy – apart from poor Sophie and Dan, but then, I suppose there are always some things you just can't plan for.

"Vi." Jack's studying his watch. "We've missed the Queen's speech. For the first time ever!" ∎

Church Stretton, Shropshire

Set in the Shropshire Hills Area of Outstanding Natural Beauty is the busy market town of Church Stretton. To the east is Caer Caradoc, with the remains of an Iron Age fort. To the west lie the upland moors of the Long Mynd. Both are popular walking routes.

Victorian visitors to the popular spa dubbed it "Little Switzerland", inspired by the local dwellings clinging to the hillsides.

The town's history goes back much further than the Victorians, though. It is underlain by some of the oldest geology in the country – the rocks in this area are over 560 million years old. They're active for English rocks, too. The nearby Pontesford-Linley Fault experienced an earthquake registering 5.1 on the Richter scale on April 2, 1990.

Earthquakes don't seem to have worried the Romans. They built a road through the area which forms part of today's A49. The name "Stretton" comes from a combination of two Old English words, "streat" and "tun", meaning "Roman road" and "settlement".

The "Church" part of the name distinguished Church Stretton from the settlements of Little Stretton and All Stretton when they were separate. The town now has four churches. Parts of St Laurence's Church date from the 12th century.

The Real Santa

by Nicky Bothoms

THE sleet fell all around him before vanishing into a wetness which slicked the pavement beneath his feet. Hunching his shoulders and side-stepping into the street, Peter strode past the other shoppers and did his best not to think unkind thoughts.

His Christmas spirit did not extend beyond that. Not at five past five on Christmas Eve when he was late to pick up his six-year-old niece from a Christmas party halfway across town because all the nearby parking spaces had filled up hours ago.

It never failed to amaze Peter how easily people seemed to lose their common sense at Christmas time. It was only one day!

Something made him remember he needed teabags. He would have to hurry if he was going to collect Lana and make it to the supermarket before it closed.

Peter turned and advanced on to the high street proper. It was a seething mass of dark winter coats broken only by the odd flash of colour from a bobble hat or scarf. And they were all heading in his direction.

The early close of the high-street shops had sent an exodus of people on to the street, all now intent on getting home with their last-minute purchases clutched under their arms.

Taking a deep breath, Peter huffed and grunted his way through, sensing his reserve of Christmas spirit dwindling further. He really wasn't sure he would have any left for the journey home with Lana.

"Come and see Santa and his reindeer! Here at half past five!"

Out of the crowd popped an elf, complete with green suit, green shoes curled at the toe and a bluish tinge around her cheeks.

Peter slid to an undignified halt in front of her.

"Eh?"

"Santa and his reindeer at half five!" She beamed, shoving a leaflet

Illustration by Shutterstock.

into his hand. The crowds streamed past on either side of them, creating a small eddy of calm.

"Actual reindeer?" was the only question that came to his mind as Peter stared at the leaflet in a daze.

"Of course! How else will Santa pull his sleigh?"

He blinked. There wasn't much to say to that, after all.

"There'll be all nine of them, including Rudolph," she added.

"Nine?" Unsure how and why he had captured the attention of this bubbly elf, Peter looked around for an escape route. Unfortunately, the crowd continued to stream past.

"Yes! Dasher, Dancer, Prancer, Vixen, Comet, Cupid, Donner, Blitzen — and Rudolph," the young woman reeled off, still with a huge smile on her face.

"Oh . . . well . . . I'll, uh, try to make it." He shoved the leaflet into his pocket just as another person emerged into the elf's periphery.

With a cheery wave, she bounded away in their direction, leaving Peter to be swallowed up by the jostling crowd once more.

Peter glanced at his watch. Quarter past five. He had already been late and now the elf had made him even later. With renewed effort, he pushed through the crowds towards the town hall, muttering to himself.

So much for Christmas spirit. It had been Christmas spirit which had got him into this! He should have guessed something was amiss when his sister had snapped up his half-hearted offer to collect Lana from her dance party.

Peter sprinted up the steps and into the lobby of the town hall. He was greeted by the sight of a forlorn little angel, her tinsel halo unravelling and the tip of one wing bent.

She was standing next to her dance teacher, who was dressed like a Christmas tree.

"Hi, Lana. Sorry I'm late." He crouched down in front of the little girl before casting a glance up towards her teacher. "Is everything all right?"

The woman nodded.

"I think so, Mr Howard." She rested a hand on Lana's shoulder. "Lana got a little upset but she wouldn't say why."

"Oh?" Peter looked back at Lana. "Do you want to tell me what's wrong?"

Eyes downcast, she shook her head.

Her dance teacher gave a slight shrug.

"Maybe she'll tell you later. She's not hurt so I imagine it was nothing worse than a silly argument." She leaned down to help Lana pull her jacket on over her wings. "We'll see you for dance class after the holidays, OK, Lana?"

The little girl sniffed but nodded.

Clasping Lana's small hand in his, Peter began trudging back down the steps of the town hall.

"Did you have a good time before you had your argument?"

Lana did nothing but shiver in her jacket. Her hand felt ice-cold in his.

"Do you have your gloves, Lana? You're freezing."

She came to a sudden halt on the steps as she wriggled her hand out of his to feel about in her coat pockets.

"There you go! It's a bit of a walk to the car because it's so busy. Everyone is getting ready for Christmas." He paused for a beat before seizing on a point which would surely summon her excitement. "Santa is coming soon!"

All at once, her little mouth turned down and her lower lip trembled, accompanied by a tell-tale glistening in her eyes.

Oh, no! Christmas Eve, heaving crowds and an upset little girl. His Christmas spirit was all but spent. He was only one man.

"Why are you upset, Lana?"

"I hate Christmas!"

Well, this was going from bad to worse.

"How can you hate Christmas?" Peter countered, striving to be jovial. "You get to spend time with your family, eat sweets for breakfast and you also get presents from Santa!"

"That's not what the other kids said!"

"What?" He began to panic.

"Santa doesn't bring the presents," she explained, her eyes growing larger by the second – and still brimming with tears. "It's just grown-ups dressing up as Santa."

"Well, it is true that some people dress up as Santa," Peter conceded. "But that's only because the real Santa is busy getting everyone's presents ready at the North Pole."

Lana looked down at her feet.

"They said it was all grown-ups."

"Every single Santa? Did they say really say that?"

"Yes."

"What do you think, Lana?" Peter knelt down on the step below her so he was at eye level with her. Her expression changed from teary despair into a confused frown.

"I don't know." She shrugged, fiddling with her gloves. "The other kids said."

Something crinkled in his pocket and he remembered the leaflet the smiling elf had given him. What had she said? Santa and all of his reindeer, including Rudolph, at half five.

"I think I can help you work out what you think, Lana." Peter grinned at her as the embers of his Christmas spirit began to flicker just a little brighter. "What does Santa have that helps him pull his sleigh?"

"Reindeers?"

"Exactly! Don't you think that the real Santa would have reindeer with him just now since he needs to get ready to deliver all the presents?"

"He wouldn't have time to go back to the North Pole since it's already Christmas Eve."

Lana gave a slow nod, finally raising her gaze to meet his. A little gleam of hope crept into her eyes.

"So, if you saw Santa and his reindeer, would you think he was just another grown-up?"

Her brow furrowed for a moment while she bit her lip, considering. Then, with more decisiveness, she shook her head hard enough to make her halo wobble.

"Not if he had reindeers. You can't be pretending if you have reindeers."

"Well, look what an elf gave me." Peter pulled out the crumpled leaflet and smoothed it out, handing it to Lana for her inspection.

His Christmas spirit burst into a flame which engulfed the tiny voice screaming at him about the cold, the crowds, the time, the parking and the teabags.

It was Christmas and a little girl had lost her faith in Santa. They made films about this, for crying out loud.

"Can you read what it says on there?"

"No."

"It says that Santa and his reindeer will be visiting here at half past five. Would you like to go and see him?"

Lana was wide-eyed.

"Santa and his reindeer will really be here?" she gasped.

"Yup, and if we go to see them, then you can decide what you think about Santa. Does that sound like a good idea?"

Her gaze was fixed on the leaflet, looking at the pictures and mouthing the words to herself. She raised her head and regarded him with faint suspicion.

"Did an elf really give you this?"

"Well," Peter began, slow and thoughtful, "she was dressed in green, her shoes curled up at the toes, and she had a hat with a bell on the end." He raised a brow. "Does that sound like an elf to you?"

He was rewarded by the first hint of a proper smile.

"Come on then, it's almost half past. We better hurry!"

What was it with Christmas and being late? The two seemed to go hand in hand.

He was going to be late for getting those teabags, too. He could only hope that there would still be time to pop into the supermarket.

It became clear that much of the crowd had dispersed even in the ten minutes since he had walked over to the town hall.

In fact, there were so few people that Peter felt his stomach lurch. Had it been cancelled? Had Rudolph picked a fight with the other reindeer? Had Santa fallen off his sleigh?

Or, more mundane but far more likely, what if he had simply missed it? His Christmas spirit dimmed in the face of such adversity.

He should have waited until he was sure that Santa and the reindeer were here before he promised Lana. This was the trouble Christmas spirit could get people into if they let themselves get caught up in it.

"Hello! Are you going to stay and see Santa and his reindeer?" A green shape seemed to materialise in front of him.

"Eh?"

The elf beamed.

"I think that's what you said before, too."

"How can you remember?"

"Because she's an elf, Uncle Pete!" Lana burst out, staring up at the elf in amazement. "She helps Santa know if you've been bad or good!"

"That's exactly right!" The elf knelt down. "Although I'm afraid that I'm not sure who you are when you're dressed up. What's your name?"

"Lana Howard."

"Lana Howard. Hmm, Lana." The elf studied her with deep concentration. Suddenly, her expression cleared into one of recognition. "I remember! You are definitely on the Nice list!"

Without warning, Lana's whole face crumpled and she burst into tears. The elf looked distraught. Peter took pity on them both: he scooped Lana up in his arms while addressing the elf.

"Some other kids said some things." He glanced down at the small number of leaflets still clutched in the elf's hand. "I was hoping that seeing Santa and his reindeer would help clear things up for her."

"Oh, I see." The elf's expression cleared and her smile resurfaced. "Well, just you wait until tomorrow, Lana. You'll see I was right!" She pointed to a line of barriers extending along the high street.

"If you stand over there, you'll soon see Santa and his reindeer."

Lana darted another glance towards the elf before looking up at her uncle.

"Does she really help Santa with his list?" she asked shyly.

"Well, she knows all the names of his reindeer," Peter pointed out. "Not many ordinary people know that, do they?"

Lana scrunched up her face with the effort of recalling the names.

"Rudolph?" she ventured at last.

The elf laughed and nodded.

"Yes, he's the most famous. But there's Dasher, Dancer, Prancer, Vixen, Comet, Cupid, Donner and Blitzen. That's nine altogether.

"I'd better go and see if Santa is ready. You'll wait by the barrier, won't you?"

Lana nodded in wonder. Hand in hand, they walked over to the steel barrier separating the small crowd from the route which Santa and his sleigh would take through the high street.

The town's Christmas tree with all its hundreds of tiny fairy lights sat at one end, while the Christmas light displays bolted on to the side of the shops cast yellow, green and red glows on the wet pavements.

A sudden tinkle of bells announced the arrival of the sleigh at the top of the high street.

The reindeer tossed their heads as the sleigh jingled and jangled along behind them, providing a pretty melody to accompany the rhythmical clip-clop of their hooves.

Peter could hear Lana counting them with careful deliberation.

Behind the reindeer sat a figure in a red and white suit complete with white beard, a tummy like a bowl full of jelly and no doubt a twinkle in his eye.

He held the reins in a firm hand whilst he raised the other hand to wave at the excited crowd. Lana bounced up and down on her tiptoes as she waved back, her face shining brighter than any star atop a Christmas tree.

Peter discovered he was excited, too. His little flame of Christmas spirit finally roared into a steady fire. He found himself recalling all those childhood Christmases when the only thing which mattered was deciding what to put out for Santa: a piece of Christmas cake or a mince-pie.

What interrupted his rosy recollections was the clanking sound of shutters being pulled down further up the street. The shops were now definitely closed for Christmas. Even the supermarket.

However, that was precisely the moment when Lana spun round and flung her arms around his waist, squeezing him tight in a hug.

"Thank you, Uncle Pete!"

His gaze fell to the little crumpled angel with her halo askew and her bent wing bent poking out of the top of her jacket.

A little dishevelled, yes, but brimming with infectious excitement once more. His renewed Christmas spirit soothed away the last of his agitation.

Oh, he would manage without his teabags until Boxing Day. It was only one day. ■

Downpatrick, Co. Down

There have been people living in the area of Downpatrick since Neolithic times. Archaeological excavations in the rolling drumlins around the town have revealed several ancient settlements.

By the time the Romans were including the British Isles on their European tours, there was an established community here. Ptolemy, the famous Greek astronomer and cartographer, mentions the town of "Dunum" in his map of about AD 140.

The Irish word *dún* (fort) refers to the fort that once occupied the hilltop site on which Down Cathedral now stands. The Ulster Cycle, stories of Ireland's deep past, talk of the warrior Celtchar who lived in a castle there. Rāth Celtchair (Celtchar's fort) was one of the town's earliest names. Later, St Patrick built his first church there.

Ireland's patron saint is believed to have lived in the town in the fifth century. After his death in AD 461, he was buried on Cathedral Hill. Down Cathedral was constructed on the spot and St Patrick's grave remains a place of pilgrimage today. The Saint Patrick Visitor Centre in the town tells the story of the saint and his influence.